Desecrated Lands

Desecrated
LANDS

A Novel by
Peter Pikkert

Essence
PUBLISHING

Belleville, Ontario, Canada

Desecrated Lands

Copyright © 1996, Peter Pikkert

ISBN: 1-896400-19-1

Essence Publishing is a Christian Book Publisher dedicated to further-ing the work of Christ through the written word. For more information, contact: 103B Cannifton Rd., Belleville, ON, Canada K8N 4V2. Phone: 1-800-238-6376. Fax: (613) 962-3055. Email: essence@intranet.on.ca Internet: http://www.essence.on.ca

Printed in Canada
by

Essence
PUBLISHING

To Basil Qaqeesh.
He was there when I needed him.

Table of Contents

✦ ✦ ✦ ✦ ✦

Introduction

✦ ✦ ✦ ✦ ✦

Desecrated Lands might best be described as an autobiographical historical novel. It is a novel in that the main characters are figments of the imagination. It is historical in that the flow of events, even many of the small details, are documented. It is autobiographical in that Jim's struggle was very much my own – a struggle which had less to do with the imprecise doctrine of eschatology, than with such unequivocally biblical teachings as righteousness, justice and mercy, and their relationship to Christian Zionism.

Though I have lived most of my adult life in the Middle East, I have never set foot in Israel. The reason is simply that I don't want to forfeit my chances to enter those Arab countries with which Israel is still technically at war. This meant, however, that I was dependent on secondary sources for my descriptive passages of Palestine and Israel. I relied heavily on George Adam Smith's classic work, *The Historical Geography of the Holy Land,* and the bi-weekly magazine, *Middle East International.* For Jordan and Syria, I drew largely from my own experience.

The historical framework was provided by Philip Hitti's *History of the Arabs*, Peter Mansfield's *The Arabs*, Colin Chapman's *Whose Promised Land?* and Thomas Friedman's *From Beirut to Jerusalem*. The Intifadeh, the Oslo Accord, the Hebron massacre, Yitzak Rabin's assassination and descriptions of other recent events are drawn from reports in *Middle East International*.

There really is an International Christian Embassy in Jerusalem, and though Ambassador Stanley Harding is fictitious, much of what he said is based on statements made in an article on Christian Zionism in the March 2, 1992 issue of *Christianity Today*.

My characterizations of Arabs are based partly on two families in Jordan, the Qaqeeshes and the Rabadis, who were to me what Akram's family was to Jim – "a surrogate family, a gateway to the Arab world," and partly on Raphael Patai's classic, *The Arab Mind*.

The glossary will help the reader understand those terms relating to Arab history and culture with which he may be unfamiliar.

I want to thank my brother-in-law William Kennedy and Dr. Michael Haykin for their invaluable critiques of the manuscript.

Peter Pikkert

PART ONE:

Reality

✦ ✦ ✦ ✦ ✦

1

Piercing Sweetness

✦ ✦ ✦ ✦ ✦

ANGER ENHANCED her beauty. "You're quitting to go back to the Middle East? What about us?" Her eyes flashed, her chest rose and fell. "These last two months you seldom wrote. What happened? Did you fall in love with some Arab bellydancer? Answer me!"

"Honey, don't be silly." Jim gazed admiringly at her.

"Don't be silly?" Her voice rose. "You throw away our future and call me silly? How can you do this to me? Jim, why? What about our marriage plans?" she pleaded.

"Honey, don't ask me why. I simply have to..." Jim spoke quietly, firmly. "I love you, Lois. Come with me..." He loved her, loved her strong character.

Her voiced changed from pleading to derision. "You quit your thesis, renege on your commitments to the kibbutz, leave school and then expect me to join you on some fool's errand? You're a fool, a quitter." She stood up, tossed back her hair and walked out. He watched her go. She slammed the door behind her. A minute later he heard the elevator open and close and begin its long descent.

For a long minute, Jim stared indecisively into space. Then he picked up the phone and placed it beside his armchair. He sat down, propped his feet on the window sill, folded his arms and stared silently over the city. Evening fell. The colours deepened, the bridge stretched its long shadow over the rose-tinted water. The streets were congested.

The phone rang. Jim reached down and lifted the receiver. "Hello?"

"Mr. Wilson?"

"Speaking."

"This is Worldwide Travels. Sorry to keep you waiting, sir. Your ticket to Amman, Jordan is confirmed." The girl on the other end hesitated. "Sir, are you certain you want a one-way ticket? Just fifty dollars more will get you a year long open-return."

"Yes, I'm certain, thank you. I'll pick it up in the morning."

"As you like, sir."

Jim replaced the receiver. He felt exquisitely alive.

Amman, Jordan

Dearest Lois,

Though I know it doesn't appear that way, I love you, darling. In fact, I love you so much it hurts. I love you enough not to marry you, as I don't want you to marry someone who shrinks back from uncomfortable truths.

It grieves me to think how I hurt you, but your respect is worth more than your love. I hope to win back your respect and resurrect your love. Honey, give me time.

My dearest Lois, an honest life is worth any price – even the price of losing you. I would be dishonest to myself, to you, to God, if I didn't pursue this quest to the end.

The joy of being re-united with you while knowing I'd hurt you grievously kept me from sharing openly about my experiences in Palestine. I feared you wouldn't understand. Let me attempt to pour on unemotional paper the complex of events and emotions that drove me to leave school, sacrifice my career and risk losing you to return to the Middle East. I pray that you will understand because, in spite of the turmoil, I wouldn't trade the piercing sweetness that accompanies the price of seeking truth for anything.

It all began one weekend on my previous trip when I'd left the kibbutz to go sightseeing...

2

Beginnings

✦ ✦ ✦ ✦ ✦

THE BELLS TOLLED as Jim left the bus terminal. They triggered a surge of emotion in him. It was as though Christ's birthplace extended him a special welcome. At the kibbutz there were no bells – only the call to prayer drifting up five times daily from the Arab village.

Following the directions in his guide book, he wound his way up to the restaurant. "A simple establishment with tasty food and low prices. Situated on the northern slope of the old town, it boasts a lovely view. Good value for money," it said.

Out of breath when he reached the place, he gladly lowered himself into a chair. A young man approached his table and poured water from a plastic bottle into a glass. As if reading his mind, the waiter said, "The water is fine, sir. I just opened the bottle."

Jim looked at him in surprise. "How did you know that I'm English-speaking?" he asked.

The waiter pointed at the backpack and smiled. "Pike's Peak is an American brand. What would you like to eat?"

Jim laughed. "What do you recommend?"

"Are you familiar with Maqlubi? It is a tasty meat, aubergine and rice dish."

"Sounds good. I'll try it."

The waiter left and Jim gazed at the serene landscape below him. He could see the spires of the Church of the Nativity rising above Manger Square. The minarets of a large mosque and the steeples of various Syriac, Catholic and Orthodox edifices also pierced the sky. Beyond the town a succession of olive orchards, fig trees and vineyards led to the white limestone hills and the deep, winding ravines of the Judean wilderness.

The waiter reappeared, carrying a large, steaming dish. "Can I get you something else?" he inquired politely.

"Maybe you can tell me how to get to the youth hostel?" Jim asked.

"The authorities shut it down," the waiter replied. "The owner's son threw stones at Israeli armored cars."

"Oh." Jim didn't know what to say.

"There is a bed and breakfast place near the market. It's cheap, but dirty and noisy." The waiter hesitated before continuing. "We also take in guests. Bed and full board for just fifteen dollars a day."

Jim raised an eyebrow. "The guidebook doesn't mention that."

"Sir, these are difficult times," the waiter answered simply. "We have an extra room and we offer Arab hospitality."

Jim wondered what they would think at the kibbutz if they learned he'd stayed with Arabs. Yet this waiter seemed different from the Arabs he'd heard about... He took the plunge.

"OK, your place is probably as good as any. By the way, what's your name? Mine's Jim." Jim stuck out his hand.

"I am Akram." The waiter shook his hand. "Enjoy your dinner, Mr. Jim. Afterwards, I'll show you where we live."

After dinner, Akram took Jim home, introduced him to his mother, excused himself and went back to work. The mother, a small lady with large, smiling eyes, showed Jim the guest room and in broken English invited him to join them downstairs after he'd made himself comfortable.

Jim made grateful use of the shower, washed some of his clothes in the sink and hung them on the balcony railing to dry. Then he went downstairs. In the living room, a man wearing a black and white kafiyeh was sitting on a lounge chair beside a kerosene stove. A cross hung from the wall above him. When the man turned toward him Jim looked into the bluest, friendliest eyes he'd ever seen.

"Welcome, son," the man said in slow, measured English. "Make yourself at home. I believe you have met our son, Akram?"

"Yes sir, I have." Jim lowered himself onto the couch.

"Are you a tourist, son?" the man asked politely.

"I'm working up north, near Rama," Jim said evasively. "I'm travelling a bit during the long weekend."

"At which kibbutz are you working?" the man asked pleasantly.

Jim's heart skipped a beat. "Kefr Giladi," he said.

"Really?" The man's eyes lit up. "That is a beautiful area. We used to go there when we were children. An uncle of mine owned the land before the Jews drove him away in '48. We used to play among his lovely olive trees – probably the very ones you are now tending."

At a loss for words, Jim stared at a picture on the coffee table. He recognized Akram, the father and the mother, but not the three other young people. Akram's father saw him looking at the picture. "That's the rest of the family," he said. "The one with the glasses is Tarik. He's in jail for throwing stones. The girl is Haifa. She is a nurse and lives in Jerusalem. The other boy, Elias, the one with the beard, studied engineering and then joined the P.L.O. He is with Yasir Arafat in Tunisia. Did you know Arafat was also an engineer before founding Al Fatah?"

Jim didn't know. Hoping to change the subject, he looked at the cross. "Are you Christians?" he asked casually.

The man smiled. "Of course! Most of Bethlehem is Christian." The man moved into a comfortable position. "There are large Christian communities in many Arab countries. In fact, some of the greatest Arab nationalists have been Christians." Jim's heart sunk; he wished he hadn't brought up the subject. "Take Butrus Al Bustani, father of Syrian nationalism and translator of the Bible," the man continued. "Or take..."

"Dad, are you boring our guest already?" Akram grinned as he entered the room.

"Not at all," Jim said gratefully. "I just wondered about that cross."

"Most of Bethlehem is Orthodox, though mum and dad are Catholic. I attend a little Evangelical church and take evening classes at the Bethlehem Institute of the Bible."

"The Bethlehem Institute of the Bible?" Jim asked incredulously. "I didn't know there were evangelical Christians here," he continued eagerly. "I myself am a teacher at a seminary in the States."

"What is an American theology professor doing at Kefr Giladi?" the father asked. Jim didn't notice the twinkle in the blue eyes.

"I'm not a professor yet, sir," Jim replied innocently. "I'm spending a year in Israel perfecting my Hebrew and doing research for my thesis."

"What are you researching?" Akram asked.

"Eschatology – the doctrine of the end times. Communism's demise and other events force us to rethink the identity of the Antichrist, the world leader who will launch the final attack on Israel..." His voice trailed off.

"And who do you suppose this Antichrist might be?" the father asked pleasantly. "An Arab?"

"Er, Saddam Hussein's attacks on Israel during the Gulf War seem to some to foreshadow that to some," Jim stuttered.

"Dad, I promised Mr. Jim Arab hospitality," Akram interrupted. "Would you attend to the restaurant tomorrow? Then I can show Mr. Jim some of the local sights."

The father laughed expansively. "Mr. Jim, Arabs love talking politics and religion. Someday you can tell me all about the relationship between the Antichrist, Saddam and America's evangelical schizophrenia..." Akram frowned at his father and Jim looked puzzled, but before they could respond, Akram's mother was offering everyone bitter coffee in tiny cups.

The next morning, Jim and Akram explored the ancient biblical sites around Bethlehem. They visited the so-called house of Joseph, explored the church of the nativity and wandered over the shepherd's fields. Jim found it refreshing to be with another Christian. There were no other Christians in the kibbutz.

They were munching on a falafel at the Well of David when Jim waged his question. "Akram, what did your father mean by America's evangelical schizophrenia?"

"He meant that we are the dupes of your unsound theology," Akram said slowly.

"What do you mean?"

"He meant that many of you American evangelicals have a double standard. Ignoring the Bible's teachings on righteousness, justice and mercy, you apply totally different standards of expected behaviour to Israel. You believe that because Israel is God's chosen people, she can do no wrong and that Israel's enemies are automatically God's enemies. He meant that your eschatology has perverted your moral system." Akram spoke thoughtfully.

"Do you not believe that the Jews are God's chosen people?" Jim need not have wondered if his question would offend.

"You don't have to be Jewish to be chosen by God," Akram replied gently.

"That's different," Jim retorted. "The Bible teaches that God has a special plan for the Jewish nation."

"Maybe," Akram replied, "but where does this urge to help God carry out His plans come from? Judas Iscariot also helped carry out God's plans yet do you remember what Christ said? 'The Son of Man will go as has been decreed, but woe to that man who betrays Him.' Why can't you just preach the good news and minister to the oppressed? That's what Christ did! You support a regime which oppresses my people because that is supposed to speed up Christ's return. That is wrong! To you, modern Israel is an extension of biblical Israel and you seem to think that we Palestinians are modern Canaanites who need to be destroyed! To you, the state of Israel seems to prove that God lives; to us, it is a creation of the United Nations on our land. Now we are fighting for what is ours, just like your founding fathers fought British tyranny."

Akram had spoken fervently. He jumped up and for some distance they walked in uncomfortable silence. Suddenly,

Akram threw his arm around Jim. "I'm sorry," he said. "I trust I didn't hurt your feelings." There were tears in his eyes.

Jim threw his arm around Akram's shoulders. "No, you're giving me something to think about," he replied pensively. "Until now, I've never thought about you Palestinians as brothers in Christ. I'd like to learn more..."

"Then talk to Father."

3

Reasonable Hatred

✦ ✦ ✦ ✦ ✦

MAYBE THE ABSENCE of women gave the place its romantic ambience, or maybe it was the dusty, smoke-filled air, the loud, animated conversations and the bubbling waterpipe. Maybe the romance existed only in Jim's mind. His eyes followed the dexterous movements of the waiter, whose amphoric tea glasses defied gravity as he swung his tray perilously through the teahouse.

Akram's father, absentmindedly sipping Turkish coffee from a demicup, was absorbed in a card game. Suddenly, the winning card landed on the table with a thump.

Father straightened up and gathered the deck.

"So you want to know more about Palestinians?" he asked, turning to Jim. "Ours is a long, depressing history," he continued without waiting for an answer. "We have been controlled by foreigners since the time of the Romans. The Arabs incorporated Palestine into their empire in the 7th century and the indigenous peoples, descendants of the ancient Phoenicians, Philistines and Canaanites, soon learned Arabic and many became Muslims."

"So Palestinians aren't really Arabs?" Jim asked.

"No more than the Syrians, Iraqis, Lebanese, Egyptians or North Africans," Akram's father said, smiling. "In pre-islamic times, the term 'Arab' referred to the camel herding Bedouins of the desert. 'Like an Arab in the desert,' says the prophet Jeremiah and Isaiah talks about the Arab pitching his tent. However, the islamization of Arabia in the 7th century triggered waves of Arab expansion out of the desert and the term 'Arab' assumed a second meaning. It began to refer to all the peoples who gave up their ancestral languages and adopted Arabic as their mother tongue.

"While the conquered learned Arabic, their conquerors became town dwellers. In time, the distinction between the conquerors and the conquered diminished and disappeared and 'the Arabs' were the predominant population in a huge area covering North Africa and Southwest Asia. An Arab today is anyone whose mother tongue is Arabic and feels himself to be an Arab.

"In any case, we Palestinians have been living on this land for several millennia and have been the majority population since the Romans deported the Jews. The Crusaders exploited us and then the Ottoman Turks sucked us dry. When the British promised us independence if we helped them defeat the Turks, we fought for them, only to discover that they cheated us as well."

"You are not the majority population anymore, are you?" Jim stated.

"We are still the vast majority in the occupied territories, though there are plans to expel the remaining 1.2 million of us to join our 1.8 million brothers already expelled."

"That can't be true," Jim said. That kind of talk sounded like Arab scaremongering.

Akram's father shrugged his shoulders. "Clearing Palestine of Arabs has been the Zionist's aim from the start. After the first Zionist congress in 1897, Theodor Herzl wrote that they would have 'to spirit the penniless population across the border.'" Akram's father smiled sadly. "In 1948, we constituted two-thirds of the population. Today, we are 40%, despite a birthrate that is more than double that of the Jews. How do you explain that? It is because we Palestinians are paying for Europe's atrocities; this land was not empty when the U.N. voted the State of Israel into existence. Believe me, I empathize with the Jews. They have suffered atrociously at the hands of you Westerners. Unfortunately, the Jews, instead of learning from their terrible history, only use it as a club to browbeat their opponents. Your chosen people, the Zionists, are aggressive, arrogant, intolerant barbarians who willingly wage war on all who impede their progress." Akram's father spoke quietly, obviously convinced of what he was saying.

"Didn't the Jews acquire the land legally?"

"Legality and justice are two different concepts. Most of the land belonged to absentee landlords. They sold it for a pittance to the Zionists. Zionist land hunger drove prices up, so local landowners began to sell as well. Then Arab moneylenders raised interest rates to 50%, forcing the small farmers to sell. Still, before partition, we were 69% of the population owning 94% of the land. Under the partition plan, we were given 48% of the land, something no self-respecting Arab could accept without a fight. We fought and lost. We fought again in '56 and again in '67 and again in '82 and we lost again and again and again. By 1987, we had no one left to fight with us and nothing left to fight with but the pavestones – which we have been using ever since. We will continue to fight and continue to lose."

"Then why go on fighting?"

Akram's father smiled sadly. "Fighting gives us dignity."

For a moment Jim said nothing, then he asked hesitatingly, "Does your being a Christian make a difference?"

"I understand, but I do not share my Muslim neighbour's reasonable hatred." Akram's father re-shuffled the deck of cards. "If you want the Muslim perspective, talk to Muhammed Karami. He lives in Jerusalem. Akram can tell you how to get there." As Akram's father began dealing the cards, his son stared at him in surprise.

4

The Temple Mount

✦ ✦ ✦ ✦ ✦

I T WAS THE FEAST of Tabernacles. The crowd surged over the Temple mount, spilled onto the roadway, then retreated unexpectedly back into an alley. Jim stumbled and fell. He screamed as people trampled over him. Suddenly, an iron grip lifted him from the pavement and dragged him to the side. Then a volley, a piercing scream and a soft blow to the back of his head sent Jim reeling again. The iron grip released him and he slumped to the ground. Jim stumbled to his feet, turned and stared at the owner of the iron hand now holding half of his contorted, screaming face. Part of the man's jaw slid down Jim's shirt. A surge of adrenalin followed a wave of nausea. Jim grabbed his saviour by the waist, draped the man's arm around his neck and they stumbled into a side street.

Staggering under Iron Grip's weight, Jim's sole concern was to get away from the shooting. Suddenly, Iron Grip fainted and slipped from Jim's grasp. Just then, a big man, his face covered by a kafiyeh, materialized out of the chaos and grabbed Iron Grip under the armpits. Together they carried the limp body through the pandemonium into another alley. A door opened and closed and they were in a courtyard. A young woman motioned toward a mattress on which they laid Iron Grip. The big man spoke a few muffled sentences through the kafiyeh, then headed back to the entrance. Jim followed, but the big man turned to him. "You stay here," he ordered, "She's a nurse." Then he disappeared.

The girl looked at Jim briefly, then said cryptically, "I'll look at you later. First this man."

Jim felt dizzy and became aware of a throbbing headache. He gingerly lowered himself onto a bench. He could hear shouting, shooting and running on the other side of the door. He was nauseous and very weary. He slumped forward, putting his face in his hands. Suddenly he jerked his hands back and stared at them. They were covered in blood. For a minute he thought he would faint, then he collected himself and went to the girl. She was busy bandaging the remains of Iron Grip's jaw.

"I have a wound to my head," Jim said. His knees were shaking.

"I'll look at you in a minute. Here, hold this knot."

Pulling himself together, Jim held the bandage while the girl deftly tied it around Iron Grip's head. Then she gave him an injection.

"There is little else we can do for him. Once things have calmed down a surgeon will have to sew him back together. Do you know him?" The girl had a soft, warm voice.

"He saved my life," Jim said simply.

The girl turned to Jim. "Let me look at your wound."

Jim sat down while the girl peered at the back of his head. "Grazed. I'll put some disinfectant and a bandage on it."

The girl looked strangely familiar to Jim. She was petite, her black curls framing tranquil eyes and a soft, kind face. She had lovely, unblemished skin. Before he could figure out where he had seen her, however, Big Man re-entered carrying a teenager. The boy, his leg dangling at an awkward angle, looked like he was in shock. Big Man deposited the boy on the bench, spoke a muffled sentence and disappeared again.

"I'll cut the trouser leg," Jim said. Together they cleaned the wound and set the leg, tying it firmly with some boards.

As he worked, Jim felt anger clearing the mental fog. He neither knew nor cared about the cause of the riot. He only knew that soldiers were shooting innocents like himself, like these two. Jim's head throbbed dully, the boy sobbed quietly and Iron Grip groaned restlessly. He felt close to these people. Iron Grip had saved his life, Big Man helped him save Iron Grip, this dark-eyed angel had patched his head and together they were saving the boy's leg. He'd never before thought of Arabs as either hurting or caring people.

The noise outside subsided. Big Man reappeared, locked the courtyard door and flopped onto the bench. Unwrapping the kafiyeh from his face, he turned to Jim and smiled.

"Did Haifa patch you up?"

Jim froze in mid-motion, his mind racing. Haifa? Haifa! That family photograph...

5

Olive Branches

✦ ✦ ✦ ✦ ✦

THE LARDER WAS sufficiently well-stocked to provide through almost any length of curfew. They whiled away the time talking, reading, playing cards and watching news broadcasts, alternating between Jordanian and Israeli stations. When the authorities lifted the curfew for an hour, they took Iron Grip and the youth to a hospital.

Akram's sister lived with Muhammed Karami. Their endeavour to break with tradition in their pursuit of social liberation had brought shame on their families and they hadn't heard from home since Haifa had moved in with Muhammed. Haifa in particular was very pleased when she learned that Father had suggested Jim visit them. They interpreted the gesture as an olive branch.

When he learned that Akram's father had told Jim to get the Muslim perspective from him, Muhammed had to laugh. "No matter how much pork I eat, the old man will always think of me as a Muslim. I'll be happy to give you the P.L.O.'s perspective though."

"Please do," Jim said.

"The P.L.O. was formed in '64 and until '67 was a tool of Arab regimes." Muhammed lit a cigarette, made himself comfortable and continued. "After the Six Day War, however, we determined to be our own masters. A number of clandestine Palestinian guerrilla groups called fedayeen took control of the P.L.O. and in '69, Yasir Arafat, head of one these groups, Al-Fatah, was elected chairman. Under him, the P.L.O. evolved into more than a liberation organization. It became our government. Besides fighting Israel, the financial aid which the Arab states gave us to do their fighting for them enabled us to run schools, hospitals, an industrial cooperative, and to establish various social services and a Palestinian Red Crescent.

"During the '70s, the P.L.O. matured from radicalism to realism. Instead of trying to 'drive the Jews into the sea,' we began fighting for a state in which Jews and Arabs have equal rights. In November '74, the U.N. recognized the P.L.O. as the representative of the Palestinian people. That was when Arafat made his famous olive branch speech," Muhammed smiled.

"By '77, we'd acquiesced to where we would accept a state anywhere the Jews were willing to withdraw from! We will accept a rump state consisting of the West Bank and Gaza, an area only 20% of Palestine. We will accept security zones, demilitarized zones, peacekeeping forces, anything, so long as we can live in peace and run our own affairs. Our mission is one of peace!" A piercing earnestness had crept into his voice.

"Strange," Jim mused. "Yours is a mission of peace, yet you triggered civil wars in both Jordan and Lebanon."

"Triggered is the right word," Muhammed replied. "Triggered implies a situation any jolt or spark can set off. The P.L.O.'s influence and organization threatened the balance of power in the Hashemite Kingdom, so in September 1970, the king drove us out. That was a sad day for the Arab nation." Muhammed's voice reflected his emotion.

"After that, our fighters settled in Southern Lebanon. Our presence there also triggered a situation waiting to explode. Remember, the Jews drove our fighters from Lebanon in '82, yet neither they nor the U.S. Marines were able to stop the Maronites, Muslims and Druze tribes from devouring each other. What chance has a gorilla got in a snake's nest? Our Lebanese brethren should thank the Syrian viper for imposing order in '91," he said dryly. "You Westerners invariably think of the P.L.O as a terrorist organization when in fact it is no more violent than any other government trying to protect its people from an aggressor."

"Tell me a bit about Yasir Arafat," Jim asked, accepting a glass of tea from Haifa.

Muhammed smiled. "We call him 'Al Khityar,' the old man. He is the ultimate freedom fighter and the ultimate politician. You Westerners have never learned to appreciate him. He symbolizes our indestructibility; that's why we love him, potbelly, popeyes and all. When the Jews crushed us, the Arabs shafted us and the world forgot us, he rescued us from oblivion. He raised us from the dead and propelled us into international orbit. He transformed us from refugees in need of handouts into a nation aspiring sovereignty. He made our cause sacred in Arab, Islamic and Third World politics. For that we will forgive him his multitude of mistakes."

Muhammed sipped his tea before continuing. "Arafat was a wealthy building contractor in Kuwait. Back in '56, however, he liquidated his assets and formed Al Fatah. Throughout the '60s, it struggled against the Jews who controlled our land, as well as against the Arabs who controlled our lives.

"As I said earlier, the '67 debacle, when Israel routed the Egyptian, Jordanian and Syrian armies in less than a week, thoroughly discredited the Arab states. They left a void into which Arafat's Al Fatah stepped by carrying out several spectacular confrontations in Israel. This so enhanced his legitimacy that he was able to wrest control of the P.L.O. from the Arab states and forge the various Palestinian factions into one independent national movement, our de-facto government. In a sense, we were co-victors in '67; before that our land was occupied by three states – Israel, Egypt and Jordan. No one can win a war against three enemies. After the dust settled in '67, however, we had only one enemy left to cope with: Israel. At that time, the U.N. Security Council also passed Resolution 242, which condemned Israel's military occupation and called for a complete withdrawal. Our struggle is perfectly legal," Muhammed smiled again.

"Actually, for a couple of decades, we teetered between total subjugation to, and all-out confrontation with Israel. Finally, they pushed us over the precipice. They shut down our schools, taking away our young people's education, their only hope. They blow up the houses of parents whose children misbehave, and break the bones, imprison or deport those they don't like. Retaliation became inevitable.

"When an Israeli truck driver got nothing more than a speeding ticket for killing 4 and injuring 17 Palestinians in December 1987, we decided to shake the yoke of oppression from us. The *Intifada*, the 'Shaking,' was born."

Muhammed looked at his watch. "Its time for the news." He stood up and switched on the T.V.

6

Arrest

✦ ✦ ✦ ✦ ✦

L IEUTENANT KAHANE, an American immigrant, looked like a scarecrow in a hurry. His uniform hung loosely over his gangly frame, the trouser legs barely covering his ankles, and a shapeless beret clung to the side of his long, sallow face. His superiors, his peers and his subordinates all secretly despised him. He was too gung-ho, he walked and talked too fast, he worked over-time too often and was too ambitious for their liking.

Lieutenant Kahane was once again working over-time. Leaning forward, his bushy eyebrows furled in concentration, he watched a video. It showed a crowd surging from an alley, stopping, then milling back in confusion. The Lieutenant pressed the "hold" button when a blond head appeared on the screen. He studied it carefully, then pressed the "play" button again. The blond man turned around, gestured toward Abu Sami, then stumbled and disappeared. The Lieutenant fast forwarded to where the blond man briefly re-appeared. Embracing Abu Sami, the two disappeared into an alley together.

The Lieutenant popped a second video into the player. It was of the same area but from a different angle. He fast-forwarded through scenes of panicking people until the blond man re-appeared. He and a large masked man were carrying the now wounded Abu Sami. The Lieutenant slowly inched through the sequence to where the large man's kafiye slipped down. The camera caught a brief glimpse of the face. The Lieutenant zeroed in on it.

"I want sketches of Blondy and this one," he said to his assistant.

Lieutenant Kahane smiled. Since the three didn't re-appear on any other video, he knew they had taken refuge somewhere in the area. Not only had he identified Abu Sami, he had discovered two henchmen and located a P.L.O. safe house. His captain's stripe was definitely in the bag.

They were eating supper when the armoured personnel carrier careened past. It was followed by the sound of rough commands, angry replies and banging doors.

"Search party," Haifa explained.

"What do they look for?" Jim asked. An ominous premonition seized him.

"Someone to blame the riot on," Muhammed replied. "Anyone whose ID card isn't up-to-date or who possesses something they consider subversive literature or a weapon. If you happen to break a broomstick that day, they'll arrest you for possessing a club."

Someone shouted something in Hebrew, then thumped against the door. Jim's heart tightened when Haifa let the soldiers in. Several men in riot gear pressed into the kitchen, one of them casually pointing his Uzi machine gun at Jim's stomach. An unusually tall officer carrying a clipboard scrutinized them closely through his bushy eyebrows.

"Bingo!" he said. Smiling, he turned the clipboard around and showed them remarkably accurate drawings of themselves. He gestured to the soldiers who promptly flung them across the kitchen table, roughly searched them, snapped on handcuffs and shoved them out the door.

"Take the bitch as well," the officer said.

When the armoured vehicle's door slammed shut it seemed to Jim to seal his doom. His breath came fast and shallow and he feared he'd wet his trousers.

Muhammed smiled wanly in Jim's direction. "You wanted the Palestinian perspective..."

Jim winced as a soldier hit the big Arab on the head and told him to shut up. Haifa sat erect beside him, skin pulled tight around her cheekbones. As the machine rumbled to life, Jim cried inwardly to God.

7

Prison

✦ ✦ ✦ ✦ ✦

O N THE FOURTH DAY, Jim decided prison was an incongruously jolly place. Dank, dark, filthy, overcrowded, yet jolly. Jolly, because imprisonment was rewarded with freedom of speech; the men could shout their colourful insults and hollow threats at the guards with lusty abandon.

The cell's front consisted of floor to ceiling bars. The thin mattresses used at night were stacked in one corner and a toilet was in the opposite corner. About 50 men were packed into his cell. Over half the inmates were under 16 years of age; there was even a 12-year-old charged with stone-throwing.

There was a pecking order among the inmates which was most evident at night – the underdogs had to sleep closest to the toilet. This ranking, Jim noticed, was not based on brute strength alone, but also on one's crime, wit, age and friends. When the soldiers pushed them into the cell, a dignified middle-aged man welcomed them, asking who they were and what had happened. When Muhammed said that Jim was an American who wanted the Palestinian perspective, the men cheered. The dignified man assigned them a sleeping place near the front of the cell, away from the toilet.

The first two days were the worst. Jim felt utterly deserted. His demands for a lawyer and access to the U.S. embassy fell on deaf ears. He despaired when he learned that the 12-year-old had been awaiting trial for over a month and that some of the men had been held for four or five months without a hearing. He began to despise these arrogant Jews who callously arrested, held without trial and tortured as they pleased.

Through his acquaintance with Akram, he'd become interested in learning the Christian Palestinian's perspectives on eschatology and the Holy Land. Learning and experiencing, however, are two different things. Suddenly, history and theology seemed irrelevant. The only reality was Jewish injustice.

By the third day, he'd lapsed into sullen resignation, but by the fourth day, the incongruous jollity of the place dawned on him.

Besides shouting insults at the guards, the men whiled away the hours, the days, the weeks, the months talking and playing cards. Jim soon discovered the extreme boredom of incarceration. The daily highlight was their hour in the courtyard.

Muhammed shaped chess pieces by dipping pieces of bread in water, shaping them and letting them dry out. He scratched a chessboard onto the concrete floor and for several days they played chess tournaments. Though most men spoke Hebrew and a number some English, Jim avoided those who talked politics or religion.

Jim did, however, develop a friendship with a cinematographer. Jemal Karim was about his own age, had studied in California and spoke excellent English. He had been arrested ten weeks earlier for smuggling a documentary on Gaza to a

French T.V. station. Together they talked about movies, sports and hobbies, and they dreamed of Big Macs, pizzas, tacos and french fries covered with ketchup. On the seventh day, Jim mentioned that he sung in the university men's choir.

"Come on, sing us a song," Jemal urged.

"I can't sing here," Jim protested.

"Why not? Sing us a song! It'll cheer everyone up," Jemal insisted. Muhammed, smiling broadly, nodded his head. "Yeah, come on, Jim, sing us song."

"I can't think of anything..." he replied lamely. Looking at the two smiling Arabs urging him to sing, he suddenly thought of Paul and Silas in prison. They hadn't needed their fellow inmates to urge them... Jim suddenly felt ashamed.

"OK, give me a minute to collect my thoughts," he said recklessly.

Muhammed and Jemal shouted for everyone to be quiet because Jim, a famous American singer, would give a concert. While the men looked at him curiously, Jim stood up, scraped his throat nervously, shot an inaudible prayer upward and began to sing:

> *Abide with me, fast falls the eventide,*
> *The darkness deepens, Lord, with me abide;*
> *When other helpers fail and comforts flee,*
> *Help of the helpless, O abide with me.*

Jim's confidence grew and his voice rang out with the second stanza.

> *Swift to its close ebbs out life's little day;*
> *Earth's joys grow dim, its glories pass away;*
> *Change and decay in all around I see;*
> *O Thou who changest not, abide with me.*

The men stared at him in mute amazement. Jim noticed that the guards were also listening. Looking directly at them, Jim sang the next stanza. His voice echoed down the corridors.

I fear no foe, with God at hand to bless;
Ills have no weight, and tears no bitterness.
Where is death's sting? Where, grave thy victory?
I triumph still, if Thou abide with me.

Suddenly something melted in Jim and the assurance of God's presence filled him, erasing the bitterness and grudging resignation. His eyes filled with tears and his heart overflowed with irrational praise. He took a deep breath, closed his eyes, lifted his hands and sang like he'd never sung before:

Reveal Thyself before my closing eyes;
Shine through the gloom, and point me to the skies,
Heaven's morning breaks, and earth's vain shadows flee;
In life, in death, O Lord, abide with me.

The tears flowed down his cheeks as he sat down. For an eternal moment time stood still. Then the men burst into noisy applause, shouting for an encore. Jim, emotionally spent, sat with his head in his hands. Jemal lifted Jim's face by the chin and looked him in the eyes.

"Thank you." Jemal's voice trembled.

"Thank you," Jim replied, wiping the tears from his cheeks.

The next day a guard came for Jim. While the man led him away to be interrogated, 50 men and boys shouted encouragements after him. As he walked down the corridor, an uncanny peace enveloped him.

8

All in a Day's News

✦ ✦ ✦ ✦ ✦

THE U.S. EMBASSY eventually arranged Jim's discharge. Muhammed, Haifa, his friend Jemal Karim, the 50 boys and men in his cell and ten thousand others didn't have an interceding embassy. They were left behind, remembered only by their loved ones.

After the man from the embassy handed him his passport, Jim walked back to Muhammed's house. He approached the place uncertainly, not knowing what to expect. The door hung loosely on one hinge. He pushed it aside, entered the courtyard and looked around in amazement. The house was devastated, a pile of rubble. Jim picked his way through the broken glass, smashed furniture and ruined household goods to the bench, sat down, hunched forward and began weeping. The cathartic tears flowed copiously down his cheeks, each wholesome sob releasing more pent-up tension. He'd been strong during the weeks of imprisonment, the interrogations, that damning video, the beating, and their insistence that he was Iron Grip's or rather, Abu Sami's, accomplice. The irrational destruction around him triggered a long overdue emotional release.

Eventually, he blew his nose, looked around sheepishly and left, gently pulling the door shut behind him. He withdrew some money from the bank, phoned Akram, ate a shoarma, signed into a cheap hotel, showered and slept. He woke up the next morning rested and hungry.

While waiting in the hotel restaurant, he turned the pages of a *Jerusalem Times* someone had left behind. Nothing had changed during his weeks of incarceration. News in Palestine was static; only Jim's experience of it was different.

"The U.N. Human Rights Commission in Geneva condemned Israeli human rights violations and the settling of civilians in the occupied territories. The measure was carried despite the objection of the U.S., which voted against it."

"The U.S. Secretary of State met with Arab and Israeli officials. The talks were described as constructive and useful."

"The Israeli Defense Forces shot dead three stone-throwing Palestinian youths on the West Bank, while a 27-year-old man was killed because he was out after curfew."

"The Israeli-supported South Lebanese Army fired heavy artillery against Hizbullah positions in South Lebanon to mark the anniversary of Israel's killing of Sheikh Abbas Musavi."

"The Israeli Air Force successfully attacked Palestinian positions in South Lebanon. Air Force spokesman Levi Shakak described the attack as a preventative measure."

"Three masked youths were shot dead by Israeli troops in Gaza while writing graffiti on a wall."

"Upon his receipt of the Jabotinsky award, the Rev. Stanley Harding, president of the Christian Embassy in Jerusalem, declared that one of the reasons God has blessed America was because it had stood with Israel. 'Israel has a biblical mandate over the land. Deportation is the most humane way for Israel to deal with terrorists and rebels,' he said. 'The Palestinians,' he added, 'have no legitimate claim to this land.'"

Jim folded the paper, ate his meal and ordered coffee. Sipping the strong, hot, sweet, energizing liquid, he realized that he had changed irrevocably during the last few weeks. It made him feel insecure. The knowledge that, like the Muslim and Jew, he was a prisoner of his own culture was unsettling.

Akram's simple statements, his father's comments, Muhammed and Haifa's bravery and his own prison experience were exposing his biases which, when confronted with flesh and blood, seemed hollow. His shallow piety and superficial moralism, his Zionism and his espousal of America as the pinnacle of providential history – his whole fundamentalist value system – was cracking and tottering. At the same time, he longed to discover a core of truth valid for both himself and his new Palestinian friends.

He stood up, paid the bill, headed for the coast road and stuck out his thumb. That longing, that hope, drove him now. Though he feared the journey, his longing for an as yet vague destination was too strong to allow a return to the past.

Before long, an old Mercedes with a smiling Arab wearing his kafiyeh at a rakish angle, pulled up. The man reached across the front seat and flung the door open.

9

Military Law

✦ ✦ ✦ ✦ ✦

E N ROUTE, Jim learned that Fayiz Hasake lived in the
Khan Yunus refugee camp, that he was a waiter in a
restaurant in the old city of Jerusalem, that he had four boys
and three girls and that he drove his old Mercedes to
Jerusalem daily – or rather, whenever the Gaza strip wasn't
sealed off. Jim also learned that Gaza is less than 50 kilometers
long and 10 kilometers wide and consists of sand, half of which
was either colonized by Israelis or sealed off by the military. He
learned that there are about 850,000 Palestinians squeezed
onto the remaining bit of land, that it had been under curfew
for about four years and that Fayiz had spent two years in
prison. Then they stopped at a roadblock. Fayiz rolled down
his window.

Three uniformed youths approached the old car. A pimply
conscript gave the door a kick. Jim's stomach tightened, no one
else reacted. The youth peered at Fayiz's papers and Jim's
passport, then ordered them out of the car. Jim noticed that the
youth's combat boot had badly dented the door.

They searched the car but found nothing. "You're getting a ticket because the back-seat passengers aren't wearing seat belts," the pimply youth said. His buddies grinned.

"But there are no passengers in the back," Fayiz protested.

"I say there are, and I say they're not wearing seat belts," the youth leered, winking at his buddies. They guffawed with laughter.

Fayiz and Jim continued their journey in silence. Fayiz seemed depressed, the rakish angle of his kafiyeh out of place. Jim stared blindly out of the window. He was disturbed. He couldn't fathom how a people who had themselves been victims for thousands of years, whose history was meant to be a symbol of hope – of slaves receiving freedom, dignity and a Promised Land – and whose laws were to become the yardstick of morality could become so brutal, so violent, so debased. The worst thing was that they seemed to blame their victims for not cooperating in the rape. Instead of remorse, they justified themselves with the casual, irresponsible attitude that the Palestinians deserved what they got. If Israel was no different from other nations, Jim thought, then hope was dead.

10

Shabura

✦ ✦ ✦ ✦ ✦

THE ISRAELIS call Rafah a trouble spot. It lay squeezed between Egyptian border fences and expropriated dunes in the southern tip of Gaza. It was the poorest and most defiant town in the occupied territories. More than half of all intifada gunshot injuries occurred in it.

Shabura was a square kilometer of 35,000 refugees inside Rafah where negotiations, elections, international debates and peace talks were distant irrelevancies. It was a place where old women searched for stones for their grandchildren to throw and where destroyed homes were flung piecemeal back at the destroyers. In Shabura, the intifada became a primal urge as necessary as food or sex.

When an army vehicle ventured on the sandy road into Shabura, a cacophony of whistles and horns would sweep through the camp, mobilizing the population. Following the fortified vehicle's movements from the rooftops and alleyways, hundreds of youths would wait. Suddenly, in response to some unseen, unheard signal the intruder received a barrage of stones, which would trigger an angry response from the guns poking from slits in the vehicle's side. The vehicle would then do a three-point turn and retreat down the sandy road, followed by a thousand hoots and jeers. Shabura's children developed such an accurate arm and such sophisticated whistles and calls that they could throw stones over houses to hit unseen vehicles driving along parallel streets.

The army once established an observation post in Shabura. The residents burnt it down. Several months later, another Star of David flapped from a new post. The battle with the army lasted the whole day. The more the soldiers shot, the more people went crazy. Eventually, the soldiers lowered their flag, got into their vehicles and shot their way out. The army hasn't had a permanent presence since. After prison, the higgledy-piggledy alleys and open sewers of Shabura were the freest place in Palestine – at least during the daytime.

It was late afternoon when Jim arrived. The acrid pall of burning tires hung over the camp. Broken glass crunched underfoot. He sensed a hundred hidden eyes following him through the crowd. The youth he asked for directions led him through the maze of alleys to the clinic. The kid refused a tip.

The clinic consisted of two rooms, a waiting room and a surgery. Waiting patiently on a rickety chair, Jim looked at a yellowing poster of a man being gunned down. The man's feet crumpled beneath him, his arms were spread out as though crucified to an invisible cross. An old fashioned rifle fell from his hand. "Why?" it asked in English in big, black letters.

The door to the surgery opened and an old man stepped out. He was followed by a mirror image of Jemal Karim wearing a white doctor's coat, but sporting a neatly trimmed Islamic beard. Jim hadn't known that Jemal and his brother were twins.

Dr. Karim invited him into the surgery. "What can I do for you?" he asked, beckoning toward another rickety chair. Jim sat down.

"My name is Jim. I shared a cell with your brother, Jemal," he said. "He is well and sends his greetings."

Dr. Karim's eyebrows lifted in surprise, then he smiled. "Thank you for the message. We haven't heard from Jemal since his arrest," he said. "Are you visiting the relatives of everyone in your cell block?" The doctor's voice betrayed his suspicion.

"No," Jim said. "Let me explain. I am an American. I came to Israel to improve my Hebrew and do research on my thesis. I was working on a kibbutz when I came into contact with some Christian Palestinians. Through them I got interested in the Palestinian issue. I ended up in prison by accident, where I met your brother. We became friends. He suggested I learn about Islam from you."

"Mr. Jim, curfew begins in twenty minutes. You are welcome to spend the night with us, then we can talk at leisure." Dr. Karim stood up. "I don't meet an American Christian who wants to learn about Islam every day," he added, smiling disarmingly. Jim marvelled afresh at the Arabs' irrepressible hospitality.

The doctor locked up and they wove through the rush of people scurrying about before curfew. The streets had to be deserted by 7:45 P.M. They came to a shanty mosque, turned the corner and pushed through a rusty steel door into a tiny courtyard. The place had the sour, familiar smell of people living too closely together without the luxury of modern sanitation and garbage disposal. An elderly lady and a teenage girl were squatting around a plastic basin rinsing clothes. They quickly stood up, embarrassed by the stranger's unexpected arrival.

"My mother and sister," Dr. Karim said. In rapid Arabic, he explained Jim's presence. The girl dragged a mattress and some pillows into the courtyard and the two men squatted comfortably.

"Surely you have studied Islam before?" Dr. Karim asked.

"If the Islam we've been taught is as far removed from the facts as the Christianity your Imams teach you is, it's no wonder we misunderstand each other," Jim smiled.

Dr. Karim had to laugh. "You're right," he said. "I admire your search for truth. Like the proverb says, 'Seek truth, even if you must travel to China to find it.' God will guide those who seek him with a sincere heart.

"Islam, as you know, means submission," he continued. "In the Kur'an God revealed His will. We Muslims seek to submit ourselves and our society to that will. This gets us into trouble with our secularized, westernized authorities who, though paying lip service to God, don't recognize His authority. They would have us reduce Islam to the five pillars: the testimony, prayers, the haj, almsgiving and fasting. These, however, ought to be the mere external evidence of a deep personal and communal submission to God. The true Muslim moulds himself to the moral character of God, who is merciful, compassionate and generous. As a community, we seek to base our society on Shari'ah, the holy law of the Kur'an. That is where we come into conflict with most Arab regimes, which are Western puppets dancing to Western tunes. It is your secular, Western value system which we Muslims cannot abide.

"What we Muslims fear from Westernization is not your technology and science but a reduction of the function of Islam to the level Christianity plays in Western society. That would leave us as spiritually and morally bankrupt as you are."

The mother re-entered the courtyard and placed a foot-high table before the men. Then she put a platter of rice covered with a watery bean and tomato stew before them. The doctor picked up a spoon, handed it to Jim, muttered "In the name of God, the merciful, the compassionate" under his breath, picked up the other spoon and tucked into the food.

"Let me illustrate my point," he continued between mouthfuls. "Your feminists have persuaded you that the sexes are the same, so you condemn hijab, our way of protecting our women – and with them our society – from sliding into your Western moral abyss. Or take Ramadan. To the hedonistic, self-centered, body-worshipping Westerner, voluntary self-control and self-discipline is a joke, so you deride our month of fasting. What is wrong with fasting, praying, almsgiving, pilgrimage?"

The doctor swallowed another bite before continuing with quiet, charismatic fervor.

"In our parent's generation, you Westerners dragged the world through two world wars, and in our generation, into the cold war and industrial colonialism. Is it any wonder we reject Western values? The morality and spirituality of Islam and its great promise of future reward is the tremendous unifying psychological and sociological force which will enable us to overcome our heritage as victims of imperialism." The doctor rhythmically tapped his spoon on the table, as if underlining the importance of his last sentence.

"Do you really believe that?" Jim asked. "Countries such as Pakistan, Iran and Sudan which apply Shari'ah aren't exactly Utopias."

"Our Islamic revolution faces tremendous obstacles, most

of which are either remnants of Western imperialism or cultural and ideological imports. But we will overcome your narrow nationalism and materialism. Of course, there are tremendous tensions in our society – we are in a process of change, a time of Islamic revolution. But the tensions and extremes of behaviour in our society today are no greater than when Europe dismantled its *Ancien Régime* during the French Revolution." The doctor smiled his ready smile. "We have a long view of history – that is why we will win."

The crisp call to prayer from the shanty mosque interrupted them and the doctor excused himself, fetched a prayer rug, unrolled it and prayed, repeatedly touching his head to the ground in submission to God. Then he put the small rug away and rejoined Jim, sitting cross-legged on the mattress.

"Is blaming your problems on the West not a cop-out?" Jim asked gingerly. "True, we made mistakes, but for how long will you blame the West for all your current political and social problems?"

"Of course we blame the West," the doctor said amicably, adjusting the pillows supporting his back. "The problems of the West are Western creations, the problems of the East are also Western creations." The doctor shouted something and his sister brought a book. "A simple look at an atlas is sufficient," he said. He turned to a map of the Middle East and North Africa and jabbed at the borders between Arab countries. "Look at all these straight lines. You drew them to divide and conquer us. A divided Middle East is easy to manipulate. You Westerners divided the Arab nation and you promised the same piece of land, our land, to both us and to the Jews. Of course, you are the Great Satan which divided the house of Islam. But God is sovereign. The intifada has triggered a great revival of Islam.

56

Our mosques are full. When life becomes difficult, people turn to God. When people turn to God, watch out!"

Defying the curfew, an insistent rap interrupted the doctor. The doctor opened the door and a masked man slipped into the courtyard. Suddenly Jim was afraid; he noticed a tendon in the doctor's neck begin twitching nervously as well. He couldn't understand the Arabic, but he knew the doctor was explaining his presence. The masked man turned and stared at Jim. The dull, cold, unblinking lizard eyes gazing placidly through the creased kafiye sent a shiver down Jim's spine.

"You are American pig. You supporter of Imperialist Zionists," the masked man said.

"I was, but don't think I am anymore," Jim said simply. His voice trembled.

"You leave early morning, or else trouble." The masked man reached into his shirt, drew a small, black pistol and pointed it menacingly. Then he opened the door and disappeared.

The doctor breathed a sigh of relief. "A Mulathim, a masked man," he explained. "They are the leaders of our desperate people. The little ones write the graffiti which announces strikes and warns collaborators. The higher ranks kill collaborators and organize attacks on Israeli soldiers. Our people worship them... You must leave right after curfew."

Just as Jim left the bus terminal, the bells began to toll. They triggered a surge of emotion in him. It was as though Christ's birthplace extended him a special welcome. In Gaza, there were no church bells; only wailing sirens, screaming, defiant children and weeping mothers and fathers.

He wound his way up to the Jerusalem restaurant and was out of breath when he reached the place. Akram came running from the kitchen and hugged and kissed him.

PART TWO:

Birth of a Gulag

✦ ✦ ✦ ✦ ✦

1

Heretical Logic

✦ ✦ ✦ ✦ ✦

Dear Jim,

I read your letter with mixed emotions. I don't need to remind you that I haven't yet recovered from what you did to me. I feel rejected, repudiated, jilted. I cannot appreciate your sudden extremes of behaviour, nor can I see what you hope to achieve through your impulsive actions. In fact, I fear that your emotional response to a series of unfortunate incidences rings of anti-Semitism. I sincerely hope that you will quickly resolve your inner conflicts and return home. There are many things in the Bible we will never understand. Who of us can fathom God's ways? If He, in His sovereign grace has chosen Isaac and rejected Esau, who are we to complain to Him that He is being unfair?

Considering your current sympathies, I don't know whether you care to know, but I went to the opening of the Holocaust Museum in Washington. It was a very impressive occasion. The First Lady sat two rows in front of me; I could see her clearly. We shook hands at the reception afterwards. Dr. Stanley Harding, president of the Christian Embassy in Jerusalem, was one of the plenary speakers. I wish you could have heard him. He spoke very eloquently about supporting Israel at a time when its enemies seek to undo the work of God. He pointed out that the recurring theme of history from Heliopolis to Haifa and from Haman to Hitler was the determination of gentiles to exterminate God's people. He emphasized that it is our moral duty to encourage Israel to re-build the temple as this will speed up Christ's return. I'll enclose a copy of the program and a newsclipping covering the occasion.

Jim, I don't know what else to write. People here, including myself, fail to understand what possesses you. In fact, they are embarrassed to talk about you with me. If you'd died, people would be condoling me, or if you'd run off with some other girl, they might share my anger. If you'd been institutionalized in a mental asylum, people's apologetic silence would likely be little different. Dad is furious and mum tells me I should be grateful that all this happened before we were married. Throwing your career to the wind is also causing your parents much grief. Remember how they sacrificed to see you through university!

Jim, I once loved you dearly. Right now my feelings toward you are topsy-turvy. Why don't you come back? We can forget this episode ever happened.

Sincerely,
Lois

Jim folded the letter carefully and laid it aside. Then he propped his feet on the windowsill and stared blindly from his flat on the mountain at the refugee camp in the valley. Divergent thoughts flitted through his mind, their heretical logic no longer shocking him.

"Opening of the Holocaust Museum in Washington... impressive occasion." Wasn't the holocaust a European tragedy? Wouldn't Berlin be a more suitable place for such a monument than Washington, where the edifice merely paid homage to Jewish political clout? Wouldn't a museum commemorating the genocide of the American Indian and the enslavement of the African be more appropriate for the American capital...?

"Ring of anti-Semitism." Is anti-Zionism the same as anti-Semitism? Are there not many Jews who are anti-Zionists? Is anti-Semitism not hatred of the sons of Shem, which includes the Arabs? Is anti-Zionism not merely repudiation of some ill-defined, militaristic political program? He didn't know whether he was an anti-Zionist or not. He did know, however, that experiencing Israeli repression had given birth to a moral outrage in him. He wanted to do something – he didn't yet know what – for his fellow victims.

"Dr. Stanley Harding... rebuild the temple... speed up Christ's return." Does supporting Israeli expansionism really speed up Christ's return? Doesn't the very concept of man speeding up Christ's return impinge on God's sovereignty? To what extent should we worry about eventual divine plans for Israel? Surely we shouldn't base our morality on our eschatology?!

"Seek to undo the work of God..." Who'd want to worship a God whose works can be undone?

"I once loved you dearly... come back..." She still loved him. There was hope.

Evening fell, and with it, silence.

2

Dieter

✦ ✦ ✦ ✦ ✦

THE FACT THAT Jim's lodgings were too expensive was a bonus. Another student invited him to share his accommodation, so Jim moved from sterile Jebel Amman, where English-speaking Jordanians drive German cars and live behind inaccessible walls, to the edge of a refugee camp on the outskirts of the city. Here, Palestinians spoke Arabic and were crowded into rough, cinderblock dwellings which throbbed with life. In this rough and tumble world, Jim determined to master the language and the culture. Here he'd forge a blood-and-tears theology of grassroots involvement. Here he'd enter into the Palestinians' felt needs.

When Jim, the last of the Baby Boomers, started high school, his new roommate Dieter commenced grade school. While Jim's parents paid his way through college, Dieter's got divorced. When Jim received his B.Th., Dieter started high school and when Jim received his M.Div., Dieter quit school. When Jim, enjoying a dilemma of opportunities, struggled to "find God's will" for his professional future, Dieter faced unemployment in an AIDS-ridden, debt-laden, concrete jungle.

Jim was gregarious; Dieter affected an androgynous, bored look. While Jim, disengaged from issues outside his comfort zone, fought polemical battles over the objectivity of truth, the certainly of knowledge, the state of homosexuals in the Church and the State of Israel in eschatology, Dieter did volunteer work during the day and lost himself in contemporary music at night. His was a jaded, disillusioned, post-Christian generation. When Jim sported custom-made suits with silk ties, carried a leather briefcase and carefully groomed his hair, Dieter sported baggy trousers, a black T-shirt, black Doc Marten boots, wore both earrings in the same ear and carried a scruffy little backpack over one shoulder.

One day, Dieter's girlfriend invited Dieter to a discussion group. The man leading the discussion talked about Jesus Christ turning his back on the political and spiritual institutions of his day to form a close-knit group of disciples that was in the world but not of it. The man said that though the authorities crucified Christ because He rejected them, God raised Him from the dead and called Him home to heaven. The man pointed out that this same Christ still invites people today to follow His example of rejecting the status-quo to form groups of people who live in loving, caring harmony with each other. The picture the discussion group leader drew of Christ touched Dieter deeper than anything else had since his parents divorced.

Though the girlfriend eventually dropped out of the scene, Dieter kept attending the discussion group and eventually integrated into the church that sponsored it. The mid-week prayer meeting exposed him to missionary work. One Wednesday evening, a guest missionary spoke about the challenge of Islam. The man sparked an interest for the Arab world in

Dieter which grew into a fascination, a passion. He began reading books on the Middle East, eating in Lebanese restaurants, visiting Arabic art exhibitions, tracking down Arabic music groups and taking evening classes in Arabic. When he learned of a youth mission working in Jordan, he approached the church elders. They were prepared to support him to the tune of a couple of hundred dollars a month, which was enough.

Dieter absorbed languages through osmosis. He spoke fluent Arabic and could make himself understood in Turkish. There were few places he hadn't hitch-hiked to in his visitation of the people who had responded to the Christian radio programs broadcast from Cyprus and Monaco. His goal was leading people to Christ and incorporating them into "the archetypal counterculture, the Church." He'd been imprisoned in Turkey and the Sudan and had been deported from Lybia and Morocco.

Initially, Dieter's bouts of glossolalia, his irregular hours and his lackadaisical attitude toward personal hygiene irritated Jim. Dieter's incisive insights, however, often took Jim by surprise, and it began to dawn on him that there was something deeply spiritual about his deceptively simple roommate.

It took some months before Dieter could wrench Jim from his grammar texts and convince him that language was learned through interaction with people. Once he caught on, however, Jim learned fast. Soon he stuck to Dieter like a shadow, learning language, absorbing culture, and acquiring a store of proverbs and parables. His homework lay forgotten while he joined Dieter in drinking bitter coffee at some tea house, laughing at a lousy Egyptian movie, or guffawing at a cheap show in some grimy theatre. They spent hours sitting on sacks of rice listening to the greengrocer talk about his native Nazareth.

The butcher showed them how to slaughter a sheep, the carpenter taught them how to operate the hand lathe and the ironmonger showed them how to forge nails. Jim's friendship with Mr. Saleh, however, proved particularly fruitful. Mr. Saleh was a truck driver; he didn't mind sharing his sweltering cab with Jim for the summer holidays.

3

Glimpses

✦ ✦ ✦ ✦ ✦

M R. SALEH'S PARENTS were '48 refugees. Mr. Saleh himself was born and raised in Jordan. He had a major in journalism and a minor in English from the University of Jordan, but due to a surfeit of Palestinians with degrees in journalism, he ended up driving a truck. He was loquacious and likeable, a mine of information.

"Hafez Al Assad, the president of Syria, plays all levels of Arabic politics toward one goal: his own survival," Mr. Saleh said. They had just spent several hours at the Ramtha-Dera border and were careening northward to Damascus, trying to avoid the numerous potholes.

"What do you mean by levels of politics?" Jim asked.

"First, there are the Arab's primordial tribal relationships, best described by the proverb, 'Me against my brother, my brother and I against my cousin and me, my brother and my cousin against the outsider.'

"Second, there is the Arab's tradition of a strong man. Our history is different from yours. It isn't a history of movements and phases ushering in new movements and phases. It isn't even the history of nation states. It is the history of a succession of strong men, of dictators and tyrants. Only a tyrant can impose order on warring clans, tribes, sects and neighbourhoods. Our golden age was the age of the Ummayad and Abbasid tyrants. We love tyrants because we need them in order to make a living. When the Hafez Al Assad flattened the city of Hamma in 1982, many of us secretly cheered him on. He restored order so that I can drive my truck in peace."

"Are there other levels of politics?" Jim asked as they veered around another pothole.

"Ever look at a map of the Middle East and North Africa? The borders consist of straight lines and acute angles which are completely out of sync with ethnic, linguistic and religious reality." That line sounded familiar to Jim.

"With the exception of Egypt and Morocco," Mr. Saleh continued, "our countries are Western creations unwanted by our masses. However, the ruling elites you Westerners installed in the political structures you left behind ensured that the straight lines and acute angles hardened into permanent fixtures. Thus, tyrants like Assad and Saddam Hussein came to rule modern states. Their clans control the military and are thus able to impose order. Arab armies don't serve the defence of the nation but the upholding of the status quo in that nation." Jim fell silent as the running commentary continued.

"We've arrived in Damascus. That building up on the mountain is Assad's palace," Mr. Saleh announced. He pointed to a large, modern mansion with big, square windows overlooking the city. Passing numerous pedestrian bridges and overpasses, they drove through the sprawling suburbs towards the city centre. At the old Hejaz Railway Station, Mr. Saleh and Jim parted company for the rest of the day.

According to a pre-historic tradition, Damascus was the first city to build a wall "after the great flood." She has seen the growth and decay of races, civilizations and religions and has witnessed the rise and passage of countless Semitic hordes. Folk etymologists take the name Damascus, *Dimashq* in Arabic, and split it into two words, *dim* and *ashq*, which means "blood flowed." Cain is reputed to have killed Abel on this spot.

At first, her location seems incongruous for such an ancient, enduring city; the site is impossible to defend and barred from the sea by the double mountain ranges of the Lebanon. The secret of her eternal youth is two-fold: trade and the Barada River, the ancient Abana. All the great trade routes depart from the suq of Damascus. The south road, leaving by the "Gates of God," takes the pilgrim to Mecca. The southwest road takes the merchant to Palestine and Egypt. The eastern road leads to Baghdad, the western road to Beirut, and the northern one to Anatolia.

The city of the Khalifs lay between three great empires, Egypt, Arabia, Persia, with the Mediterranean behind and the desert before her. The socialist experiment of the 20th century stifled the city's commercial aspirations for some decades, but since the introduction of economic liberalization, Damascene merchants have reoccupied their leading place in society. Politicians come and go; commerce is forever.

The Barada river, sweeping down from the Anti-Lebanon to the west of the city and running for 10 miles down a narrow gorge, bursts into seven streams which water the vast oasis on which the city is built. Once, the gardens around her provided a rich harvest of apples, pears and peaches. Today, the

71

expanding city is fast gobbling up the remaining greenery, while the Barada, her spirit broken, disappears somewhere in a concrete tunnel.

Jim passed high-rise apartment buildings, shops selling electrical appliances and furniture, fruit and vegetable stands piled high with produce and numerous restaurants offering French, Italian, Damascene and Aleppine specialties, until he reached the heart of the old city.

He made his way to the Suq al Hamadiye, the covered market, the only place offering relief from the chilling stare of the Presidential palace on Mount Qasiun in the middle of the city. Jim turned his back on the unblinking, omniscient gaze of the large, horizontal windows and escaped from its reach in the welter of narrow, winding streets around the Ummayad Mosque.

No one with a love for the Levant can resist the old city of Damascus. Each new day begins an hour before dawn when the muezzins, many of them chosen because they are blind and thus unable to see down into the private courtyards from the tops of their minarets, rouse the people for their morning prayers. Two muezzins sometimes sing the call to prayer in beautiful, delicate harmony: "Come to prayer. Come to security. God is great." An hour later, when the morning is still fresh, the old city spills out onto the streets. The bazaars and the coffee-houses open their doors and display their wares. Merchants push their donkeys through the crowds, street vendors cry, beggars beseech and craftsmen make their artifices under their customers' suspicious eyes. In the labyrinthine market, there is a street for the gold and silversmiths, another for the jewelers and copper workers, another for leather workers, and others for potters and dyers. A mélange of exotic spices perfumes the still, heavy air. Here and there, a shaft of sunlight pierces through the rusting sheet-metal roofing, illuminating the maze of dim, narrow corridors.

Jim walked through the dusky tunnels savouring the aromas of walnut wood, bales of tobacco, carpets, scones, tawny sweets and piles of melons and mandarins. But more than these, the variety of human flesh fascinated him. The pale townsmen; the swarthy farmers; the proud Druze; the negroes; the squat Turks; the tall Kurds; European and Japanese tourists draped in cameras; wives of diplomats practising the delicate art of haggling with their favorite merchants; U.N. personnel on leave from Lebanon; Gulf Arabs, their wives hidden behind black leather masks and visiting Yemenis, their wives' colourful clothing showing seductively through slits in their black chadors; all mingled together, creating an unwitting banquet of living, moving colour.

Jim found the Straight Street, Ananias' house and the wall from which Paul was lowered to safety. He entered the great Ummayad Mosque to pay homage to John the Baptist's body, then he walked around the edifice until he found the section of wall which once formed part of the Cathedral of John the Baptist. Above its southern, bricked-up portal, he found this prayer preserved in stone: "Thy Kingdom, O Christ, is an everlasting Kingdom and Thy dominion endureth for all generations."

Eventually, Jim tore himself away from the old city and made his way to Yarmouk. Yarmouk is different. Instead of cobbled streets, stone courtyards and gnarled Eucalyptus trees shading ancient tea houses, Yarmouk has wide roads flanked by drab tenements and neon-festooned stores. Yarmouk is the home of the largest concentration of Palestinians anywhere. Yarmouk began when 100,000 Palestinians, freshly driven off their ancestral lands by the Jews, arrived in 1948. They set up camp in a small district outside Damascus. Eventually, the city's planned sprawl swallowed Yarmouk – swallowed it, but could not digest it. A generation of expulsions – the Israeli expulsion of '67, the Jordanian expulsion of '70, the '82 Beirut expulsion and the '91 Kuwait expulsion – bloated Yarmouk's population to a quarter of a million. Like European Jewry of old, invisible chains confine the Palestinian to his ghetto.

Yarmouk is the epitome of the Palestinian conundrum. Reminded daily of its impotence against Western hegemony and Israeli colonialism, the Syrian regime encourages the Palestinians to cling to their identity and fosters their hopes of return, of revenge. Yet the regime knows return is impossible as it would result in its own destruction – it would inevitably lose any war with Israel. Yarmouk means radicalization and marginalization.

Jim slowly deciphered a garish banner decorating an overpass in Black Rock, the heart of Yarmouk: "Syria struggles with you in the liberation of Palestine." Yet it was the Syrian, not the Israeli, who brutally drove the P.L.O. out of Lebanon in '83, he thought. And when Saddam Hussein lobbed ineffective scuds at Israel, Yarmouk was crawling with secret police ready to nip any pro-Iraqi demonstration in the bud. During the moment of truth, the regime sided with the West, thus with Israel. Yarmouk is the geographical expression of social fratricide.

Jim slowly walked back to the railway station. He found Mr. Saleh snoring soundly in the cab of his truck.

✦ ✦ ✦ ✦ ✦

The Damascus-Beirut road is bisected by two narrow mountain ranges flanking the Beqaa Valley. Though Lebanese, this flat, fertile valley was Syria's forward line of defence against Israeli positions and the pro-Israeli Lebanese Forces which controlled the area between Beirut and the other side of the mountain range.

Jim stared with vague interest at the dour Syrian soldiers manning cinder block checkpoints and the ubiquitous, self-important plainclothes men with pistols tucked in their trouser belts. The sinister radar installation overlooking the road seemed an extension of that cold building which stares silently over Damascus.

They sped past Zahla, a Christian town in the largely Shi'ite valley and ascended the second range. Once upon a time, the journey from the conservative Arab city to the Francophone Lebanese capital took three hours. Today, checkpoints and searches have doubled travel time.

"I used to love Beirut," Mr. Saleh started. "Old Beirut was a wonderful, cosmopolitan mix where the artist, the poet, and the political refugee were as welcome as the businessman, the armsdealer, the whore and her pimp. Sin was the norm and money could buy it all. Beirut was our Hong Kong." Mr. Saleh looked wistfully for a minute. "Even during the early war years Beirut remained Beirut."

"What happened?" Jim asked.

"That's a complicated question," said Mr. Saleh. "The first round of the civil war broke out in '75 and lasted until the end of '78. That round was primarily between the Maronite Phalangists in East Beirut and the Palestinians in West Beirut. The extent of actual Lebanese versus Lebanese fighting was limited. That round didn't destroy the fabric of Lebanon's society nor its infrastructure. The main confrontation line, the so-called Green Line, ran right through the city centre, separating the combatants. During periods of calm, many Muslims would cross to East Beirut to work and vice versa. Many Lebanese believed that their state could be put back together once all the 'outside agitators' were removed.

"The country's dismemberment happened in early 1984, and not by outside agitators at all. The Lebanese themselves wielded the butcher's knife with their own hands. The event which triggered this national suicide was the war for control of the Shouf Mountains. The Phalangist offensive against the Druze in the Shouf ignited the Druze's tribal feelings of solidarity and self-preservation. The Druze-Maronite fighting became a massive blood feud. In fact, the only kind of fighting the two sides seemed capable of was the massacre.

"That war unleashed a virus that infected the rest of the country. The Christian-led Lebanese army attacked the Shi'ites in West Beirut to try to stop them from aiding the Druze, so the Shi'ites attacked any Christians that crossed their path while trying to take control of as many Beirut neighbourhoods as they could from the Lebanese army. When the Sunni Muslims saw the Druze and Shi'ites encroaching on their turf, their militiamen tried to preserve a corner of their own, leading to confrontations with the Shi'ites and the Druze. Soon Beirut was in a war of everybody against everybody else and the outsiders – the Israelis, the Syrians and the Palestinians – were on the sidelines. It was Lebanese killing Lebanese. No matter what your political views were, you could be killed just because your identity card labelled you a Christian or a Sunni or a Shi'ite. Consequently, safety meant seeking shelter with one's own sect, in one's own religious canton."

They drove on in silence. Mr. Saleh's business took him all over the city. They drove through the derelict wasteland of central Beirut. They crossed the gutted, infamous Green Line and made their way past the windowless, roofless Fayadiya barracks where General Aoun's forces made their last stand. Their truck joined a long line of cars at the Syrian checkpoint at Jamour and passed Baabda castle, from which the General withstood the Syrian army for two years. They inched through a crowded suq, entering a deserted, once lovely Christian quarter. They passed another former battlefield where Druze, Syrians and the Lebanese government once battled Maronites, Phalangists, Amin Jemayel and Aoun's troops.

They turned onto the potholed ringroad and stopped beside a forlorn camp on the outskirts of the city. Jim looked up questioningly. Mr. Saleh smiled. "This is Shatilla," he said. "That sports field is a mass grave," he added, pointing to a muddy area. "I'll pick you up here at about 8 o'clock tonight." Jim climbed out of the cab and smiled gratefully. Mr. Saleh knew intuitively what Jim sought.

Jim entered the camp through its sole entrance, under the gaze of several Syrian plainclothes police officers. He picked his way down the pockmarked alleys and over piles of rubble, garbage and twisted metal to the sports field. Several boys were listlessly kicking a deflated ball around a rusty goalpost. A withered bouquet of flowers dangling from the goalpost by a yellow ribbon was the sole indication that this was a mass grave.

Jim sat down on a cinder block. Women trudged by with pails of water. Shabbily-dressed men shuffled listlessly to a tea house to play backgammon and talk of politics and their olive groves back in Palestine. Their once fit bodies had turned flabby and their once sharp minds were dull. Teenagers without a future strutted about playing dangerous knife games. The place smelled of sewage and despair.

Jim's head was pounding. For the first time, he realized how thin the veneer of civilization is and how quickly it can erode. A deluded man in the right place can trigger the process.

Many shared Menachim Begin's dangerous delusions – his cabinet, hundreds of thousands of his countrymen and even more evangelical Christians worldwide. They all thought the "Palestinian Problem" consisted of Arab terrorists who murdered Jews and refused to accept the Jews' divine right to their land. Since these terrorists called themselves "The P.L.O.," it was the Palestinian Problem. If one could eradicate the P.L.O., so ran the logic, one would eradicate the Palestinian Problem with it. The thing to do was simple: Just send Israeli tanks to southern Lebanon and Beirut, since that was where the P.L.O. was located. So Begin, deluded by visions of himself as the man who would create a secure and united Eretz Israel, commanded his tanks northward.

For the first time, the P.L.O. faced an Israeli army head to head. The Israelis overran the ragged P.L.O. forces in no time and had Israel not chosen to avoid entering West Beirut, the P.L.O. would have been routed in a couple of days. But for the Palestinians, that was irrelevant; winning or losing as such was irrelevant. Fighting, alone, gave them dignity. They were on the verge of their first heroic moment and they were ready to fight to the finish. Beirut would be their Alamo, their Stalingrad...

Then Arafat decided to pull out of Beirut. When he did, something died in every Palestinian. With his retreat went their dignity. Once again the Palestinians faced the hollowness of Arabic rhetoric and illusions.

The Israelis seemed to be on a real winning streak. They had scattered the P.L.O. and installed their puppet, Phalangist leader Bashir Gemayel, as president of Lebanon. However, a bomb blew Gemayel into mince-meat, to which the Israelis decided they'd better respond fast. Breaking their promise to the U.S.A., they sent their troops into West Beirut to wipe out the remnants of the P.L.O. They then surrounded the Sabra and Shatila Palestinian refugee camps.

On September 16, 1982, the Israeli high command invited their Christian Phalangist allies to enter the camps and massacre the inmates. While the Israelis sealed off the camps, the Phalangists went to work. Pregnant women had their wombs sliced open and young girls their breasts cut off. Children were decapitated and men had their throats slit. The slaughter continued for three days. No one counted the dead – bulldozers simply pushed the corpses into hastily dug holes. A quarter of the dead weren't even Palestinians – they were poor Lebanese Shi'ites who had moved in from the countryside.

Jim looked down at the muddy ground. Hundreds of skeletons grimaced a meter or two below him. She, whose moral codes revealed at Sinai formed the basis of Judean-Christian morality and ethics, she who was to be the conscience of the world, a symbol of hope, proved to be a vicious old bitch, no different from the rest of the pack. Tears welled up in Jim's eyes – not for the victims but for the victor.

"Beirut is a sad city," Mr. Saleh said. Their truck was careening southward down the coast road; traffic was light. "Seventeen thousand people disappeared during the war. Have you heard about Beirut's basement graves? They'd fill a basement with bodies, then pour in concrete. Both Muslims and

Christians did it. Lebanon is full of bitter parents whose children lie entombed under some rubble pile." They slowed down for a Syrian checkpoint. "It's a good thing the Syrians came and restored order," he added, nodding to the soldiers. They crossed the Awali river and stopped for a Lebanese Army checkpoint. A lethargic soldier accepted a carton of Marlboroughs and waved them on.

"In Old Beirut, history and beauty met. It had wonderful architecture and great markets; it was paradise on earth," Mr. Saleh started reminiscing again. "The war destroyed much, but the reconstruction is destroying even more. Skyscrapers are taking the place of the suq, hamburgers compete with shoarmas and concrete is replacing stone. The only exceptions are those parts of the city Druze leader Walid Jumblat controls. That man has good taste. I know a nice restaurant overlooking the Shihabi Amir's palace which he restored. On our return, we'll have mezze there."

They stopped at the Red Crescent in Sidon and unloaded several large crates of medical supplies. No one seemed to know what to do. An official eventually signed their papers and offered them tea and oranges. The man seemed overworked and harried – probably because he was willing to accept some responsibility, Jim thought.

They continued towards Tyre, passing a U.N. position manned by Scandinavians. A blue-beretted Nordic giant glanced at their papers, then nodded them on. You could tell from their skin colour how long they'd been in Lebanon – old-timers were bronze, new-comers lobster red. They pulled into Tyre and made their way to the Imam Sadr foundation where an attractively-dressed, friendly young woman invited them to have supper before unloading. Jim learned from her that the foundation was named after its founder, Musa Sadr, who also founded the Shi'ite resistance movement, Amal. According to Mr. Saleh, the man disappeared mysteriously back in '78. Jim was struck by the clean facilities and efficient organization of the orphanage and primary school complex. After supper, they unloaded the truck and drove to Mr. Saleh's favourite hotel. Mr. Saleh had a favourite hotel in every city.

The view from their fourth floor room was breath-taking. Below lay a scattering of tin roofs called Burj al-Shamali, yet another Palestinian refugee camp. Beyond it rose Tyre's scattering of modern high rise buildings behind which a large, red sun sunk into the scarlet waters of the Mediterranean.

He looked at the squalid camp below him. For its thousands of people, another ordinary day was over. They had laughed and cried, married and mourned, begotten and buried. A muezzin droned the evening call to prayer, a child cried, a dog barked. Jim flopped onto the bed, said a prayer for the crying child and fell into a restless sleep. Mr. Saleh was snoring peacefully.

A dull explosion rudely cut short the muezzin's morning call to prayer. Jim shot out of bed and onto the balcony. A siren pierced the early morning air. Suddenly, a distant lick of fire flashed over the blood-red Mediterranean, followed by a second explosion and another lick of fire and another explosion and another and another... Jim stared transfixed at the warship. It was aiming at something southward. A large fire broke out over the horizon. Black smoke belched heavenward, starkly etched against the soft, rose-tinted sky. The gunboat ceased firing, turned slowly, then rapidly increased speed and disappeared, leaving nothing but its bow wave to mar the smooth waters. Jim turned to see first one, then a second, then a third helicopter appear over the hilltops, fire several missiles in rapid succession toward the column of smoke and disappear from whence they'd come.

"Good morning, Israel," said Mr. Saleh. "I think it's time for us to go. Refugees will soon be crowding the road."

Jim looked at the sprawl of tin roofs below him. Children were crying and dogs barking. To beget, to bury, to forget...

"Come on, Diet, let's get something civilized to eat."

"Jimmy! Welcome back! Hey man, where've you been? How'd you and Mr. Saleh make out?"

"I've been everywhere and we got along great. Come on, man, and I'll tell you all about it over steak in the Holiday Inn."

"Steak in the Holiday Inn? Hey man, that's bad stewardship."

"Listen, for the last month I've lived on kebab and grapes. Get moving you miser. It's on me."

4

Life and Death

✦ ✦ ✦ ✦ ✦

Dearest Lois,

Much love from the Land of Revelations and Truth. Yes, this place has an uncanny ability to confront you with uncomfortable yet liberating truths; no wonder all monotheistic religions have their roots here.

"What in this world is worth dying for?" That agonizing question hounded me as I stood over the grimacing corpses of Shatilla and watched the Israeli army bomb a peaceful village to hell. Again that question tugged at me like the arid East wind did when I gazed over this land from the Golan Heights. This is the Holy Land. It is also a land of blood and gristle, of life and death, of crucifixion and resurrection. It is a desecrated land, yet it incessantly confronts you with that which matters: life, death, truth and faith.

Life and death. They are meaningless without each other and we don't really discover the former until we're confronted with the latter. What is worth dying for is worth living for, because life is truth plus faith. What are truth and faith? Truth is incarnate in the divine Son of Man who died to take away the sins of the world and faith is intimacy with Him who liberates us to die for that which is worth living for. Truly, death is nothing less than the precursor of life. Abundant life follows death like harvest the buried seed.

Honey, the callous, cruel, Chosen People have chosen to kill their half-brothers, whose blood cries from the ground, whose blood will be a precursor to new life. Honey, I will not be satisfied until I witness resurrection life where there is spiritual, social and physical death.

Dearest Lois, you asked me to "come back, to forget this episode ever happened." I cannot return to the sterile world of theological polemics. Like Christ, I want the Word to become flesh in me and I want the Spirit to blow life, abundant, throbbing life, through me to the walking dead. I want to be a peacemaker in a crimson land. I want to pray and strive for the peace of Jerusalem. Lois, my love, I want to be a missionary to a dispossessed people living in a bloody land – even if it kills your love for me.

That death is the price I am prepared to pay for life. But, darling, before you snuff out your love for me, I challenge you to come, to taste, to see, to experience this desecrated land yourself. It will enable you to intercede intelligently for me.

With all my love,
Jim

Jim folded her response carefully and put it aside. Then he tipped his chair back, put his feet on the window sill, and gazed at the camp below.

"Throw your bread on the waters and it will return to you"; "seek God's Kingdom first and the rest will be given you." He let out a long, satisfied sigh.

5

Her Visit

T HE POLICEMAN stamping entry visas looked admiringly at the elegant, black-haired girl in the trim business jacket and skirt. When her lips smiled questioningly and her innocent green eyes looked into his, his heart lurched. He received a jolt when their fingers touched as he handed her her passport back. She turned, carelessly tossed back her long, silky, black hair and walked away, leaving him staring at her exquisite legs.

"Dieter, there she is!" Jim waved furiously. Lois waved back through the thick safety glass before lifting a compact Samsonite suitcase off the conveyer belt. Her skirt swirled as she strode confidently past the customs officials.

"Jimmy, she's... awesome." Dieter gazed at her in silent adoration all the way home.

✦ ✦ ✦ ✦ ✦

While their travel permits for the West Bank were being processed, they sat on sacks of rice while the greengrocer told her about his native Nazareth. She nearly gagged when the butcher showed her how to slaughter a sheep and she admired the ironmonger's muscles when he demonstrated his ability to forge nails. Mr. Saleh told her all about the royal family and Mrs. Saleh cooked mansaf, a huge mound of rice, yogurt sauce, pine nuts and chicken, which they ate by hand.

They laughed at a lousy Egyptian movie and guffawed at a cheap show in the grimy theatre. He showed her the ancient mosaics of Madaba. He led her through the cleft mountain into rose-red Petra, that fascinating basin where the hands of man and nature combined to carve incomparable shrines, tombs and treasuries from the mountain sides.

One balmy afternoon, they climbed Mount Nebo. They stood hand in hand on its summit and gazed over the Dead Sea and Jordan river into the Holy Land. The setting sun scintillated off Jericho's rooftops and etched Qumran's cliffs against a royal-blue heaven. A warm, gentle breeze rustled her skirt and rippled her hair.

Jim looked at the beautiful, strong woman who could be his. He struggled to contain his emotions.

"I love you, Lois..."

"But not as much as your little adventures." She put her finger on his lips before he could object. "Tomorrow we enter the promised land," she said, squeezing his arm. Then she led the way down the gentle slope.

The brackish Jordan river disappointed her. They tramped across the rickety Allenby Bridge and were cordially greeted by the Israeli occupying force. The soldiers frisked them, searched their baggage and checked their papers. One of them stamped an Israeli entry stamp on a separate sheet of paper and absentmindedly waved them through. The soldiers seemed pre-occupied with a news program on the radio.

They took a taxi to Bethlehem. The morose driver listened to a Hebrew news program all the way. When they got there, Bethlehem was strangely quiet.

"Akram will come running out to meet us," Jim predicted as the taxi climbed the north slope to Akram's house. They paid their fare and got out. The street was deserted. Jim banged the door, then opened it and shouted a greeting. Akram, Akram's father and mother and half a dozen other friends were glued to the T.V. set. Akram gestured for them to come in and be quiet.

They arrived just in time to see President Bill Clinton standing on the White House lawn. They saw him stretch out his arms. Then a familiar character in khaki and kafiye, beaming through his stubble beard, held out his hand. Time stood still. Finally, a sour-faced Yitzak Rabin reluctantly reached out and shook hands with Yasir Arafat.

The men broke into loud discussions and Akram's mum shuffled to the kitchen. Time resumed its course.

6

Released

✦ ✦ ✦ ✦ ✦

USING AKRAM'S HOUSE as their base, they spent the next week exploring and sightseeing. They visited the Church of the Annunciation in Bethlehem, they travelled up to Nazareth to visit Joseph's workshop and they went down to Hebron to meditate in the mosque of Abraham. Then the letter announcing Haifa's release arrived.

The following day, they closed the restaurant, squeezed into Akram's father's old Toyota and drove to Arad Junction. Prisoners released from Ketziot in the Negev desert are invariably taken by bus to Arad Junction, the point where the Beersheba to Hebron road intersects the Tel-Aviv to Arad road. From there, former detainees are expected to make their own way home.

The drive through the fecund fields and orchards appropriated from Palestinians back in '48 takes a couple of hours. It was a pleasant, balmy day. Everyone was in good spirits. Father told stories from his boyhood and mother amazed everyone by winning a word game. Akram crooned Um Kalthum's *Ahaat*, an endless succession of ecstatic "Ahs," and

Jim impressed Lois by winning Akram's father's oral history quiz. Confessing that he'd just read Hitti's *History of the Arabs* only slightly tarnished his feat.

Arad Junction is an open, deserted area dominated by a solitary askew payphone. They piled out of the car and stretched their legs. Akram unloaded the cardboard box and his mother spread its contents on the blanket she had unfolded along the side of the road. Jim and Lois collected twigs to start the barbeque which Akram's father was fanning with a flap ripped from the box. They impaled spiced chunks of meat on thin steel rods and made shish kebab.

Every time a bus approached, they jumped expectantly, but each vehicle rushed by, leaving a stifling trail of dust. The letter said she'd be released at 11 a.m. They calculated that she would arrive at Arad Junction around noon. By three, they were getting restless. At four, Akram went to the phone booth and phoned their lawyer. He promised to look into the delay and phone back. An hour later, the payphone rang. "The bus is leaving the prison now," he said. "She'll be there in an hour and a half."

"Good grief," Lois cried in frustration. "Why can't these people keep their promises?" Father, mother, Akram and Jim first looked at each other, then at her, and then they burst out laughing.

"What are you laughing at me for?" Her feelings were hurt.

"You just asked a question that we've been asking our whole lives," Akram's father said gently.

Another bus drove past. It suddenly skidded to a halt several hundred meters past the intersection. As the bus revved into gear and continued its journey, Haifa came bobbing cheerfully down the road, her hair bouncing. Then she saw her father and froze. Father opened his arms slowly and she ran into his embrace. The lost daughter had returned home. They wept.

During the drive back home, Haifa passed on greetings from friends still in detention, entertained them with stories from prison and asked a thousand questions about family and friends. She seemed content, squeezed close to her father. Months of sitting around the Negev had given her a lovely tan. In an incomprehensible way, Lois envied this girl who lived on the cutting edge.

7

The Desecrated Land

✦ ✦ ✦ ✦ ✦

O F THE TWO HILLS, Gerizim is the more famous histori-
cally, but Ebal is higher and with the better view. From its
summit, Nablus, ancient Shechem, lies at your feet toward the
South. The eye then passes over Gerizim and 24 miles of hilltops. Westward, the range drops by irregular terraces to the
Plain of Sharon, which, though undulating, looks flattened
from Ebal's height. Beyond the plain lie scintillating dunes and
the azure Mediterranean.

Joppa lies 33 miles southeastward, Caesarea, 29 miles
northwestward. Northward, the long ridge of Mount Carmel
runs for 35 miles from its summit to the low hills separating it
from Ebal. Between Ebal and the hazy hills of Galilee lies
Esdraelon, the valley also known as Armageddon. Seventy-five
miles toward the northeast, beyond the valley of Jezreel, the
glistening mass of Hermon stands like a distant sentinel. Its
shoulders sweep southward into the Hauran above the Lake of
Galilee, merging into the skyline of Gilead and Moab, today the
Hashemite Kingdom of Jordan.

The Jordanian skyline, on the same level as Ebal, seems unbroken except for the incoming valleys of the Yarmouk and Jabbok. Though only 25 miles away, it is separated from Ebal by a wide chasm, along the bottom of which the invisible Jordan meanders into the slimy Dead Sea, earth's lowest point.

From Ebal's peak, the most famous scenes of history are visible. Jim marvelled at the influence of so small a country on the world. He wondered how the aloof, waterless plateau below him sustained the people who taught the nations about righteousness and justice and from which the Saviour of mankind emerged. It boasts no harbour, no rivers, no convenient market, is quite infertile and lies on the road to nowhere.

He trained his binoculars on the hills below. The lighter shades became ripening wheat fields and the darker shades olive groves. Suddenly, he could see Gideon's 300 men blowing their rams horns. Barak and Deborah's army sprang to life. Amos and Jeremiah were penning their visions of chaos in the wilderness along the Dead Sea coast. There, where each valley resembles the next, David narrowly escaped from Saul. Jim turned and saw Herod's battlement at Caesarea, its white temple glistening in the sun. The ruins on Gerizim became a fortress guarding the splendid city of Samaria. The sound of trumpets rose from Solomon's garrison. John the Baptist thundered judgement down below...

Lois gazed longingly at the seductive waters of the Mediterranean. She wanted to get away from this Arab family and sign into a comfortable hotel. She wanted to swim, to rub her body with lotion and to splay out on that beach. More than anything, she wanted to get off this stupid hill and take care of her blisters.

Haifa looked at the Israeli settlements dotting the countryside. A distant siren drew her gaze toward an army convoy entering Nablus. She saw little dots encircling it. She barely heard the dull crack, but clearly saw the dots scattering erratically. A lump filled her throat, a cold hatred her heart.

Jim's binoculars settled on a little Greek church in the glen below. It covers the well where Christ once told a worn-out woman that God must be worshiped in spirit and in truth. He lowered the binoculars, blew his nose and wiped his eyes. The girls looked at him in surprise.

8

The Ambassador

✦ ✦ ✦ ✦ ✦

L OIS HAD ARRANGED the interview at the Christian Embassy weeks in advance. On the appointed day, she insisted they leave extra early to ensure they'd be on time for the appointed hour. Since the bus traversed the 7 kilometers to Jerusalem in record time, they were left with an hour to spare in which to explore the City of Peace.

Jim morosely lugged Lois' camera bag from one supposed holy place to the next; he had no appetite for his appointment with Ambassador Stanley Harding. When he suggested they might go and see Haifa's ruined house, Lois decided it was time to head for the embassy.

A smiling security guard frisked them and a vivacious American girl showed them into the meeting room. Dr. Stanley Harding, radiating energy and vision, bounded in a few minutes later. He welcomed them heartily, shook their hands vigorously, offered them chairs and sat down himself.

"Permit me first of all to thank you for the generous contribution accompanying your request for this interview," he began. "God's work is dependent on the faithfulness of His people; we praise His name for the many stalwarts who support the work of the Christian Embassy." His friendly blue eyes smiled brightly as he continued. "If I remember correctly, you are interested in learning something of the historical and theological background to today's events, isn't that right?" he asked.

"Yes, that's right, sir." Lois reached into her purse and pulled out a small cassette recorder. "Would you object if I recorded our conversation, sir?" she asked timidly. Jim looked at her in surprise. He wasn't used to seeing her timid.

"Of course not," the ambassador said gregariously. He made himself comfortable and began. "The biblical vision for Israel first received popular recognition through the labours of John Nelson Darby, founder of the Plymouth Brethren. He perceived that God has one set of purposes for Israel and another for the Church. His pre-millennial view, which evangelicals today hold almost universally, emphasized the rapture of the Church and the return of the Jews to the promised land.

"Prophetic conferences, the efforts of D.L. Moody and the Scofield Bible further established the dispensational view of a literal homeland for the Jews. Then, just over a century ago, those early Christian Zionists began forging their ties with politics. In 1891, a man named William Blackstone urged President Harrison to convene an international conference to, as he put it, 'consider the condition of the Israelites and their claims to Palestine as their ancient home.'" With delicate finger movements, the ambassador indicated where Blackstone's quote began and ended.

"Blackstone's vision was endorsed by hundreds of Christian and Jewish leaders, as well as by congressmen and business leaders like J.D. Rockefeller and J.P. Morgan. It is interesting to note that Blackstone's efforts actually began before those of Theodore Herzl, the father of Jewish political Zionism!" The ambassador's eyebrows rose significantly and he nodded amicably before continuing.

"The Balfour Declaration of 1917 was the apex of Christian Zionism. Mr. Balfour, a former foreign secretary and prime-minister of Great Britain, used his clout to push through a proposal for a Jewish homeland. Together with Christian and Jewish Zionists, he persuaded President Woodrow Wilson to support his declaration, which promised the Jews a homeland in Palestine after the First World War."

"Didn't Britain promise Palestine to the Palestinians at the same time?" Jim asked gingerly. Lois glanced irritatingly at him. Ambassador Harding smiled coolly, transferred his warm gaze to Lois, ignored the question and kept talking.

"The Second World War holocaust triggered massive support for the Jewish nation and in '48, the United Nations passed a resolution supporting the creation of the State of Israel. Ancient prophecy was fulfilled and continues to be so today. We are privileged to be counted among those of whom the prophets spoke." The ambassador smiled happily.

"The '67 war, during which Israel captured Jerusalem, Judea, Samaria, Gaza and the Golan Heights drove home afresh the biblical vision for Israel. After that, no one could doubt that we are living in the incredibly exciting days just prior to Christ's return," he continued. "Indeed, the recent influx of almost half a million Soviet Jews raises the eschatological expectations of every Bible-lover. We're expecting a million more returnees from the diaspora in the coming years..." The ambassador rubbed his hands in anticipation.

"Sir, how do you feel about the Gaza-Jericho plan?" Lois asked.

"Of course we denounce the Gaza-Jericho plan," the ambassador replied frowning. "Deportation of the terrorists and rebels remaining on land divinely promised to the children of Abraham is the most humane way for Israel to deal with them." His voice rose. "Those people rejoiced when Iraqi missiles rained down on us! They have no right to this land! The root of the problem is the Arab nations' unwillingness to welcome the Palestinians in spite of their huge land holdings!"

The ambassador collected himself and continued calmly. "Our mandate at the Christian Embassy here in Jerusalem is to facilitate the return of the diaspora, to fight anti-Semitism and anti-Zionism, and to keep the biblical vision for Israel alive. That vision will culminate in the rebuilding of the temple. Thus Israel is paving the way for the second coming of the Messiah. He will reign in righteousness right here, just up the road! Think of it!"

The ambassador looked at his watch and sat forward, placing his hands on his knees. "We do not in any way seek to proselytize God's people," he said intimately. "Indeed, no one can point the finger to a single Jewish person converted to Christianity as a result of our efforts." Ambassador Harding smiled happily, then sprang upright.

Lois shook the ambassador's hand and thanked him profusely. Jim jumped up and ran for the door. He thought he was going to be sick.

9

AIPAC

✦ ✦ ✦ ✦ ✦

"CAN'T YOU BE MORE original?" Lois asked that evening. "Scheming Jews pulling strings... That's anti-Semitic hogwash."

"Don't confuse anti-Zionism and anti-Semitism. We are also Semites," Haifa said. "Have you heard of AIPAC?"

"The America-Israel Public Affairs Committee? What about it?"

"It holds your country in a stranglehold."

Lois laughed sarcastically. "We do have laws governing lobbying, you know."

"That's what you think! Woe to Israel's critics. If it wants to, AIPAC can hound your senators and congressmen out of office. It even caused the downfall of Foreign Relations Committee chairman Percy because he said that Arafat was more moderate than other Palestinian leaders! Your politicians have gotten the message long ago. In the face of Israel's daily violations of human rights, their silence is deafening."

Lois sat up. The other side of the story was disquieting. "How can they do that?" she asked.

"Scheming men pulling strings. A private meeting or a telephone conversation usually suffices. If it doesn't, labeling the candidate 'anti-Semitic' will. Listen, a politician has no chance against AIPAC, and its media allies the *New York Times*, the *New Republic*, the *Washington Post, Near East Report* and a host of other magazines and newspapers. You know how they circumvent your precious lobbying legislation? By setting up a plethora of different groups who all support the same candidate. There are over a hundred of these pro-Israeli political action committees pumping millions into the campaigns of choice candidates!"

"What is the U.S. government supposed to do about it?" Lois asked, piqued.

"Don't be so naive," Haifa responded. "Only the U.S.A. can curb Israeli misbehavior since only it can enforce disciplinary action. The U.S.A. could reduce the 10 million dollars a day of aid it gives Israel and threaten U.N. sanctions. The Russians, the Europeans and the Third World would eagerly support any American action to curb Israeli misbehaviour. Why should Israel be exempted from obeying U.N. regulations and international law? If there is to be peace in the Middle East, in the world, it will be in spite of the U.S.A.!"

Lois rolled on her back. "You will never understand," she thought irritably. "We know Israel is God's chosen nation and we know that this accord is merely the false peace before the coming of the anti-christ."

She turned to Akram's father. "Sir, how do you feel about the accord between Israel and the P.L.O.?" she asked gingerly.

Akram's father peered over the top of his newspaper. "I feel as though the thief who robbed me of a million dollars promised me ten dollars compensation," he said quietly. "But because it has been a long time since he stole my million, I will accept the ten dollars." She noticed that the kind, blue eyes were moist.

10

Jericho

✦ ✦ ✦ ✦ ✦

JERICHO VIES WITH DAMASCUS for the title of oldest continually inhabited town on earth. In any case, it is undisputedly the lowest town on earth – the Dead Sea is just down the road.

Jericho never resisted the Israeli occupiers. In fact, since its walls first fell to Joshua, it hasn't resisted any of its invaders. It never withstood a siege, no great warrior was born nor any heroic deed done there. Since time immemorial, its people have been irrigators grubbing in the soft earth. Its fame lay in its date palms and balsam wood.

The Greek Orthodox Church runs the monastery on the Mount of Temptation which overlooks Jericho. A wonderful example of 19th-century Greek architecture, it clings like a swallow's nest onto the rocks high above the city. Tradition states that the Holy Spirit led Jesus here to fast and meditate for forty days, after which Satan tested Him.

From the monastery balcony, Jim and Lois could see the whole town: the refugee camps, the Israeli settlements, the oasis, the elaborate irrigation system, the banana plantations, the modest market around Ain al-Sultan street and their hotel, the once luxurious Hisham's Palace. Jericho has a typical small-town atmosphere.

The signing of the Gaza-Jericho plan seemed to have left Jericho's inhabitants wondering how they came to be "chosen" as the first to be "liberated." The historic handshake's most tangible results were a few limp, home-made Palestinian flags hanging here and there. People didn't know what to expect. No one knew how much of Jericho was included in the Gaza-Jericho scheme and no one believed the Israeli settlers would leave.

"Once the Jews returned to the promised land through this ancient city," Jim exclaimed ardently, "and today it is their half-brother's turn."

Lois dropped his hand and turned the other way.

The next day, they crossed the Allenby bridge and re-entered Jordan. She left for the States two days later. She had been uncharacteristically quiet and withdrawn those last couple of days.

11

Shrunken Gods

✦ ✦ ✦ ✦ ✦

JIM WAS RAISED IN a narrow evangelical subculture whose fusion of conservative Protestant ethics, narrow religious devotion and "American Way" middle-class up-bringing taught that the good triumphs and obedience is rewarded. An amalgam of culture and faith forged by decades of material abundance, it taught that upward mobility in an expanding economy is God's normative blessing for America.

A product of his environment, Jim was pro-family, pro-Republican and pro-life. His theology provided no satisfying answers to injustice and the suffering of the innocent; it didn't need to since concern for the environment, minority groups and economic justice were not on the agenda anyway.

Both Dieter and Palestine assaulted Jim. Their mere presence confronted him with other, different realities. Dieter's disgust with the good ol' U.S.A. confounded him, while Palestine confronted him with the fact that God's Chosen Nations were joined together to perpetuate gross injustice.

Though Jim shrank back from these other, different realities because he feared the changes they might demand of him, he was also convinced that there must be a satisfying answer to every honest question. In the end, he rose to the challenge and determined to pursue the truth.

He began reading authors his professors had critiqued: Gutiérrez, Moltman, Metz. They posed questions his "American Way" theology never asked: Can we believe in the righteousness of God in an unjust world? What can we believe about God in a society that crushes the poor and marginalizes their humanity? What is the meaning of the Church for the oppressed? Is the common good more important than the acquisition of private property? What is the Christian response to social outrage? Is it right to take up arms to bring about social justice?

These 20th-century prophets told him to define his religion in a social context, rejecting church-world dualism. They taught him to "view from below," with the suffering, the excluded, the oppressed. They taught him to see the poor as artisans of a new humanity. They said that theology has to be done by committing oneself to the renovation of society on behalf of and alongside the oppressed. They pointed out that Christ was a manual labourer who preferred the poor, surrounding and identifying himself with the suffering, the excluded and the oppressed, and whose vision of the Kingdom of God included liberation from hunger, grief and contempt.

Jim also became obsessed with the news. He devoured newspapers and magazines. He followed the labyrinthine Middle East peace negotiations and watched the Israeli army re-enforce its positions on the ground. He felt the changing mood when September 13, the day the Oslo accord was to be implemented, came and went. He became frustrated as Yasir Arafat caved in more and more to Israeli demands, causing his credibility to plummet. He saw Rabin play the hapless P.L.O. chairman like an angler wearing a fish down by drawing the line tight and then relaxing it just before breaking point. Like hundreds of thousands of Palestinians, his initial jubilation at the signing of the Oslo accord in Washington changed to sullen, morose pessimism.

He traced a malevolent objective behind Israel's stalling maneuvers – they were turning their erstwhile enemies into modern Gibeonites, hewers of wood and drawers of water. Like the Spartans dominating their helots, Israel strove to become a 20th-century warrior race with its subjugated Palestinian serfs doing the manual labour. Jim began to understand the virulent hatred of Hamas, Islamic Jihad and other rejectionist groups. Every concession eroded Palestinian self-respect. The injustice of it all consumed Jim. Only radicals, he realized, walked tall.

Though he didn't realize it, his spiritual roots were unable to nourish him outside their own environment. His devotional life withered and his appetite for the Bible dried up. He would sit in his room, brooding for hours on end. His body hunched over at times, at other times thrown far back as he propped his feet on the window sill, he wrestled with the problem of God's chosen people – his home church, his native country and Israel – perpetuating evil.

It took several months, but by the time the Hebron Massacre took place, Jim was spiritually bankrupt, his faith dissipated. He felt betrayed, deluded. How could he serve God while witnessing His total lack of concern?

12

Purim, 1994

✦ ✦ ✦ ✦ ✦

D R. BARUCH GOLDSTEIN and ambassador Stanley Harding had many things in common. Both were doctors. Both believed that Palestine is the Jews' biblical birthright. Both believed that Israel is the fulfillment of God's promises and has a unique place in God's future plans. Both believed all nations of the world are obliged to bless the children of Sarah and curse the children of Hagar. Both believed that the Messiah cannot arrive before the Dome of Rock has been replaced by a temple. Both believed that the end justifies the means. Only Dr. Baruch Goldstein followed his beliefs to their logical conclusion.

At Purim, the Jewish people celebrate the killing of Haman the Ammonite before he could massacre the Jews. Purim, 1994 fell on a Friday during the month of Ramadan, the month of fasting for Muslims. About 700 men, women and children were kneeling in the Mosque of Abraham in Hebron, their foreheads reverently touching the floor. Suddenly, Dr. Baruch Goldstein, dressed in his Israeli army uniform, appeared from behind a mosque column and opened fire with an automatic rifle. The soldiers outside didn't interfere. Eventually, a young Palestinian struck the doctor on the head with a fire extinguisher when he tried to insert a fourth magazine into his rifle.

Fifty worshippers were killed and seventy wounded. Dozens more were killed in the riots that followed.

When the news of the massacre reached them via the B.B.C., Jim jumped up and, in a burst of frustration and anger, picked up the transistor radio and slammed it against the wall. Then he and Dieter stared silently at the pieces, shocked by Jim's violent and unnatural outburst. Slowly big, cathartic sobs began shaking Jim's shoulders and he slumped onto the couch.

Dieter sat down beside him, threw his arm around Jim's shoulder and held him tenderly. "Jimmy," he said gently, "only idiots shrink their God. You're a big idiot."

Jimmy looked up at him questioningly. Tears rolled down his cheeks.

"Don't you understand?" Dieter asked. "The God of Abraham, Isaac and Jacob will pay any price to get what He wants; and what he wants is people crying out to Him in desperation. At long last you are exactly where He wants you to be."

13

Lois

✦ ✦ ✦ ✦ ✦

D URING THE PRICE COLLAPSE of the dirty '30s, Old Man Campbell bought some of the choicest properties in town. He'd waited patiently until the post-war boom and then financed much of the downtown re-development. Old Man Campbell's son, Lois' father, eventually inherited his father's real estate empire. He had diversified the business, enabling them to absorb the shocks of the '70s and '80s unharmed. The Campbells were an old, distinguished family, well-known in town.

Only child Lois did post-graduate studies at the local Christian university, the same university where Jim was a junior lecturer in the theology department. One sunny afternoon, a mutual friend introduced them to each other on the tennis court. They played a couple of sets, after which he bought her a drink. She liked him immediately. He was intelligent, articulate, athletic. She liked the spring to his step and the twinkle in his eye. She'd accepted his invitation to the theatre.

Their relationship developed unhurriedly, naturally. Her parents liked Jim and his parents adored her. Their engagement had been a quiet family affair in an exclusive restaurant. Their wedding, however, was to be a grand occasion. Besides family and friends, father Campbell planned to invite his employees and business associates to a gala event which would reflect Campbell stature and splendor. It was to have taken place upon Jim's return from his study leave in Israel.

Jim, however, had come back a changed man. He had become testy and morose, and two weeks after his return, had stated his intention of going to Amman to study Arabic. He had left soon after, leaving Lois among the ruins of her dream castles. She was humiliated, her father was incandescent with rage.

She hated, yet loved Jim's steady stream of letters. She hated them because they eroded her security, confronting her with issues beyond her experience; they made her feel guilty. Yet she also loved them because they restored her respect for Jim. She respected his honesty, his integrity. That was why she agreed to go to Israel.

The trip was a disaster. Those camps and Jim's detailed historic explanations increased her vague, undefined guilt feelings. Because of that Palestinian family – Akram, Haifa, the mother, the father with his blue, untroubled eyes – Palestinians weren't mere terrorists anymore; they had taken on the form of a lower middle-class Christian family trying to make ends meet.

The interview with Ambassador Harding in Jerusalem had helped; maybe the Arabs really did deserve what they got! She'd been glad to get back on that Royal Jordanian flight home.

In anguish of spirit, Lois wandered over the glistening pavement. The dirty, driving rain streaming down her face mixed with her salty tears and blurred her vision.

She tried to wipe the T.V. pictures of the dozens of dead and dying in Abraham's mosque from her mind. She had recognized the spot from where Dr. Baruch Goldstein had fired – she had stood there herself.

In her mind's eye, she followed the T.V. camera from that horrible image to Ambassador Stanley Harding's pious face. "The Jews are not a normal people," the ambassador had said. "Their eternal uniqueness lies in the covenant God made with them at Mount Sinai. Thus, while God required other nations to abide by abstract codes of justice and righteousness, such laws do not apply to the Jews." The camera panned the carnage in the mosque again while the ambassador continued. "Due to God's help, Israel is stronger than all other nations, so Israel need not fear future wars. In fact, it can even provoke wars of liberation in order to obtain its promised heritage. Let us not forget God's commands regarding Amalek!"

When the interviewer asked what this "Jewish heritage" needing to be liberated was, the ambassador held up a map in which the area to the west and south of the Euphrates, including Syria, Lebanon and parts of Iraq, Saudi Arabia and Kuwait, were shaded in light blue.

"Since the root of Arab hostility is theological in nature, the conflict cannot be resolved politically. By fighting the Arabs, Israel carries out its divine mission to save the world. Like all anti-Semitism, Arab hostility springs from mankind's recalcitrance against being saved by the Jews," the ambassador had concluded.

The camera then showed some Palestinian teenagers carrying off one of their buddies. The boy's head bobbed up and down willy-nilly, blood streaming from his exposed brain. The soldier who fired the fatal shot re-loaded, aimed and fired again.

With horrid fascination, the ambassador's racist justifications rang through her head. The horrific consequences of what he said struck her with blinding clarity. She had felt claustrophobic, had thrown on her coat and walked the wet streets, enveloped in the swirling mists of her unsteady emotions. From the utmost depths of her spirit welled a plea for God to have mercy on her, a self-satisfied sinner.

14

Evil, My Ally

✦ ✦ ✦ ✦ ✦

L OIS OPENED THE ENVELOPE rapidly, ripping the stamp in the process. Her eyes flitted from line to line.

Dearest Lois,

I'm a fundamentalist fool, Christ's spittle blinding me. He'd touched me, but, unwashed, I saw men walking like trees. Focused on the temporal, my vision distorted, I failed to see the eternal. Like the Muslim and Jew, I sought God's Kingdom on earth.

I returned to Palestine dreaming of social righteousness based on divine guidelines. What folly! Like Dieter said, I'd shrunk my God and never realized it until that lunatic massacred those innocent people in the mosque of Abraham. Only then did I begin to understand what Christ meant when he told Pilate that God's Kingdom is not of this world.

Honey, God laughs at our desperate attempts to dam the tossing sea with puny legislative dikes. Instead, He allows us to choke in the mire until we give up in despair. Blessed are those whom God chooses to leave to their own devices until they give up striving. Only they who are brought to the end of their resources find rest.

I doubted divine righteousness and love because God lets the innocent suffer and die. Yet at the same time, He readily paid the ultimate price to buy some of us back from eternal death. The ultimate price! The awful, eternal God condemned the second person of the Trinity to hell to force open heaven's gates for us. But even that is not enough! He then needs to drive us, blind cattle milling helplessly in a burning barn, through that open gate! Blessed is the divine whip whose blows open our eyes to the reality of this present world.

He who orchestrated the agony of the Son, continues to orchestrate the agony of the millions for the sake of some. Evil will increase, increasing despair, the gateway to life. Indeed, the ultimate price isn't the final price of the atonement – that won't be revealed until the day of judgement.

Is it not sovereign grace when some, brought to the end of their resources, cry out to Him, whose abounding love, grace and righteousness are manifested in the divine torment of Calvary? What can separate us from a love which will go to any length and pay any price, even going so far as making evil its ally? That kind of love demands worship and compels holiness and glad obedience. It humbles yet elevates, motivates yet gives perfect rest. It answers a thousand questions yet leaves you asking "Why me?" for eternity.

Dearest Lois, my gaze is lifted beyond time, beyond politics. Honey, pray for me. I long to be like Christ, trekking through the towns and villages of Palestine, identifying with the poor and dispossessed, teaching and preaching the good news of the heavenly Kingdom. Dieter and I are about to take our first step on this new journey. We will return to the West Bank next week. We have *offered our services to the Bethlehem Institute of the Bible where Dieter will help renovate their old building and I will teach English. My hope and prayer is that my Arabic will soon be good enough to help with their off-campus Bible courses. I want to disciple God's chosen ones. Honey, pray for me. I have so much to learn. I need to master Arabic, feel comfortable in this culture and, more importantly, have people of this culture feel comfortable with me.*

Honey, I long to hear from you. I love you so much it hurts.

In God's love,
Jim

Tears filled her eyes, rolled down her cheeks and fell onto the paper, creating little round wrinkles. She read the letter again and again, then kissed it ardently.

Jim opened the envelope rapidly, ripping the stamp in the process. His eyes flitted from line to line.

My dearest Jim,

Forgive me. Forgive my selfishness, my dishonesty, my self-induced blindness.

Thank you. Thank you for not giving up on me. Thank you for praying, for writing. Thank you for your integrity. Thank you for returning to Palestine. Yes, I, whose pride was wounded, who felt you'd humiliated me, now thank God for your obedience!

Oh honey, your example and your letters were a constant, inescapable irritant urging me to analyze what I believe, as they confronted me with uncomfortable truths, truths I shrank back from. As you know painfully well, I ignored, I rationalized, I justified the way things were because honesty means change and for me, whose life lacks no good thing, change could only be for the worse. Jim, now I know why it is easier for a camel to crawl through a needle's eye than for a rich man to enter the kingdom of heaven. Now I know why the rich young ruler went away sad. We wealthy ones cannot afford to change – we have too much to lose. So instead of conforming our lifestyle to the truth, we change our religion. Instead of responding to Christ's "Follow me," we become the establishment.

That horrible massacre of those innocent Arabs in Abraham's mosque also opened my eyes. The fact that that happened exactly where we had stood several months ago suddenly made "the world out there" seem very relevant. I know this sounds very existential, but it was as if scales fell of my eyes. When the news commentator interviewed Ambassador Stanley Harding afterwards, the awful consequences of what that horrible man preaches nearly made me ill. I ran from my apartment and wandered the streets for hours, crying to God for mercy for myself, my church and my nation.

I don't know whether Karl Marx's charge that religion is the opiate of the proletariat is true or not; it is certainly true for me, Miss Bourgeoisie. I faithfully attend my comfortable church, listen to glorious music from the pipe organ, look at the beautiful lighting through the stained-glass windows, sing harmonious hymns and listen to a smooth, soothing message. All the while, I affirm that which is structurally evil: our wealth, our value system, our economic self-interests.

My dearest Jim, at long last I understand what motivates you. I love you for attempting to break out of the system. But how can *a fish fight water? How does one fight one's culture? What can we do? What can I do?*

A first step is to help you, the man I love. Precious Jim, let me pray for you as you go to the towns and villages of Palestine, teaching and preaching the good news of the heavenly Kingdom. Let me love you and learn from you about living pure and unsullied in a structurally evil system. Let me support you financially as you lose yourself that many may be found.

My dearest Jim, confronting myself has been painful. I like my comfort and wealth. Yet I want to be free to do what is right. Pray for me. Pray that God will gently loosen the ties which bind me to my world.

With tender love,
Lois

Jim smiled as he gently placed her letter in his Bible. The letter was very much the Lois he loved – strong, sensitive, a bit extreme – but then, hadn't he become rather extreme himself?

He tipped his chair back, placed his feet on the window ledge and looked out of his office window. Across the valley, he could see the Jerusalem restaurant. From the Institute basement, he heard hammer blows. Dieter was renovating the plumbing. The students would return after the Easter break.

He was happy.

15

Return

✦ ✦ ✦ ✦ ✦

O N MAY 13, 1994, Jericho woke up to a huge Palestinian flag fluttering in place of the Star of David from the roof of the police station. During the night, 400 men of the al-Aqsa Brigade of the Palestinian Liberation Army had crossed the Allenby bridge and taken up positions in the police station in the town centre, in the former headquarters of the Israeli Defense Forces, at a synagogue and outside every government office.

Once they'd gotten over the shock, the people danced in the streets and flocked from one Palestinian army unit to the next to pose for pictures. The newly arrived soldiers appeared somewhat befuddled at being back in their homeland carrying loaded automatic weapons. Palestinians from outside Jericho flooded the city. Parties continued until late at night. Young men gave guided tours of the former army headquarters and civil administration offices, pointing out the rooms where they had been interrogated and tortured.

The Palestinian Liberation Army issued no orders and made no statements. The absence of a Palestinian government

created a temporary vacuum, but since the heads of depart-
ments were all Palestinians anyway, they stayed on the job.
Several days later, hundreds of Gazans also celebrated the
return of their "children from the diaspora."

Formal control of Jericho and Gaza was eventually handed
over to the nascent Palestinian National Authority in a simple
ceremony. "I wish you success," said the Israeli Defence
Force's General Ilan Biran, while the Chief of the Palestinian
Police, General Nasir Yusuf, told the crowds that the transfer of
authority was "a historic day for the Palestinian people, the first
step on the way to independence."

The Israeli army evacuated its last installation at the old
Governor's Mansion in Gaza in typical intifada style, firing a
ritual salvo of tear gas. The Palestinians, led by their police,
then stormed the building in a fusillade of celebratory
machine gun fire.

3:15 P.M., Friday, July 1, 1994. The sun beat down merci-
lessly as Yasir Arafat stepped onto Palestinian soil. He inspected a sweltering phalanx of 400 Palestinian soldiers and waved
to a wilting 1,000 man delegation. Then he sped along the
Rafah-Gazah highway in a limousine followed by a chaotic train
of cars, buses and pick-up trucks loaded with excited youths
waving Palestinian flags. Modest numbers of women lined the
road clapping and shrieking.

Yasir Arafat filled the following days with speeches and
press conferences. He told everyone what they wanted to hear.
In Jabaliye, birthplace of the intifada, he promised the crowds
that he would not bargain over the fate of Palestinians still lan-
guishing in Israeli jails. He told Hamas supporters that he
wouldn't rest until their spiritual leader, shaikh Ahmed Yasin,
was released. "He is the shaikh of us all," Arafat shouted. "We

will not rest until he is at our side!" He thanked his "Arab brethren" for "adopting the Palestinian cause," and he told the Israeli public that he recognized their holy sites in Jerusalem. He told the press that "the most important challenge for us is to build the new Palestinian authority which will lead to an independent Palestinian state, our democratic state, a state for free persons, a state for democracy, equality and non-discrimination." He candidly told 10,000 supporters jammed into a schoolyard that the Oslo accord "is a bad agreement, but it is the best deal we could get in the worst situation." He bent over backwards to reach out to his political opponents, urging unity among the Palestinian factions. "Help lift the burden with me," he pleaded.

True to character, he earned credit by embracing danger. While other P.L.O. leaders, unwilling or afraid to assume responsibility for an agreement they helped negotiate, lounged in Tunis, Arafat addressed mass meetings in such Hamas strongholds as Rafah and Khan Yunis, paying special tribute to the injured and the families of those who had sacrificed their lives during the seven years uprising. It was still too early to notice how out of touch Arafat was after his 25-year absence.

The world reacted predictably. The Rabin government sighed with relief at the absence of inflammatory statements, and the West, pre-occupied with genocides in Africa, ethnic cleansings in Europe and mortgage payments, naively hoped that the Palestinian Problem was finally solved. After the initial excitement, the most striking reaction among the Palestinians themselves bordered on apathy. They had danced for Saddam Hussein, they had danced for the Madrid Agreement, they had danced again for the Oslo Accord and now they were too worn out to dance any longer.

Like most Palestinians, Jim and Dieter followed events on television. From Akram's parents' living room, they watched Arafat, voiceless from too many speeches, croak yet another sentence and swear in the members of the Palestinian National Authority in Jericho.

"What do you think of it all, sir?" Jim asked as Akram's father turned the T.V. off.

Akram's father answered slowly, thoughtfully. "According to Palestinian tradition, a guest is honoured for three days. After that he is treated normally. Our people, tormented by 27 years of military occupancy, will soon start to demand bread and butter from Arafat. How can he deliver? What can he promise the tens of thousands of the Palestinian diaspora?"

16

Friends

✦ ✦ ✦ ✦ ✦

A KRAM, HAIFA AND THEIR father and mother became Jim's surrogate family. They were his gateway to the Arab world. He often spent his evenings at their house or with Father and Akram in the tea house. He grew to love this family. The fact that they were Christians made their suffering and their response to it all the more relevant. Through them, he began to absorb an understanding and appreciation of Arab culture.

Father was respected in the community. His grey hairs and gentle blue eyes framed by a kafiye held in place by the black cord of the igal gave him a dignified, aristocratic, Bedouin look. Like sun melting butter and hardening clay, suffering affects people differently. Akram's father was severe, stern, authoritarian, yet his sense of honour and dignity was tempered with an unusual gentleness, a gentleness born from much suffering.

Jim tried to understand the depth of the wounds inflicted by sudden uprooting and scattering on a people who had lived on land cultivated by their ancestors for centuries. Father was thirteen in July, 1948 when the Zionist soldiers herded the entire population of Ramleh into the fields outside the city. There they ordered everyone to throw their personal valuables into blankets; those who refused were shot on the spot. About 100,000 Palestinians in Ramleh, Lydda and surrounding towns lost everything that day. Then for three days, the soldiers herded the thousands of people like cattle over the hills and through the valleys, driving them far from the roads and into the vast, barren, undulating countryside. Many died from the heat, from exhaustion, from despair. Father's sister died in childbirth. They wrapped her body in some cloth and dug a grave for her and the baby in the rocky soil with their bare hands.

Eventually, some Arabs met them, loaded them into trucks and drove them to Ramallah. There they lived for several years in a U.N. tent. They learned that two Jewish families had taken over their family home.

Father found work as a waiter in a restaurant in Bethlehem. Later, he married the owner's only child and thus inherited the business. He once showed Jim the keys and ownership papers of their house in Ramleh.

The mother, loving and compassionate, unwittingly opened Jim's eyes to a thousands little facets of Arab culture. Her immense store of proverbs and ready-made phraseology reflected many of the values Arab society instills on its own from birth. "Better to die with honour than to live in humiliation"; "be content with a piece of wild celery, but don't be obliged to someone else, O my soul"; "pass in front of your enemy when you are hungry, but not when you are naked"; "to each moment its decision"; "God cuts the cold to the size of the blanket"; "caution does not avert the decree of fate"; "the provision of tomorrow is for tomorrow." Patience, the character trait which made their lives bearable, was particularly extolled:

"Patience demolishes mountains"; "a patient man sees freedom"; "God is with the patient."

Akram was sensitive, artistic. Through him, Jim came to appreciate Arab art, music, theatre and above all, Arabic language and literature. At first, Jim marvelled at the fact that Akram could be intoxicated, reduced to tears or elevated to mystical heights by an Arab orator reciting poetry on television. As his knowledge of the language grew, however, he began to appreciate the rhythm, the rhyme, the sonorous words, the exaggeration, the over-assertion, the vast vocabulary and the repetition which, when skillfully combined, produces the "lawful magic," Arabic's ability to penetrate beyond comprehension to impact directly on the emotions.

Akram's hobby was painting, but not in a Western, representative style. As though reality to him was of such ephemeral, or possibly repulsive, nature that it wasn't worth representing, he concentrated on traditional Arabic decorative art. Using a number of basic geometric forms and patterns such as the circle, the square, various polygons, the checkerboard and the swastika, Akram painted repetitions of intricate and complex patterns which he combined with a symmetry superior to anything found in nature. Akram's works impressed Jim with their unity which, when he inspected it closer, almost magnetically drew him to analyze the interplay between the individual units. But even more than Akram's abstract art, Jim admired his calligraphy. The seemingly endless horizontal chain of letters would be interrupted rhythmically but at indefinite intervals by vertical strokes and elongations of certain letters which gave the line an inner rhythm. Jim suspected that Akram's love for abstract art, for music, for Arabic's mellifluous rhetoricism was his way of escaping the awful reality of daily life. In his own way, he was able to create something new, something beautiful, out of nothing.

Haifa was different. She had a vitality and strength of character which was a source of both pride and grief to her parents. After graduating from nursing school, she started working in a clinic in Arab East Jerusalem. She campaigned for women's liberation and abortion on demand. When she and Muhammed Karami, a nominal Muslim, fell in love, she did something few of her peers dared – they started living together. In doing so, she attacked two cornerstones of the Arab social edifice: subordination of the child's ego to that of the father; and the protection of the virginity of unmarried females. She had caused her family to lose face, to lose honour. The only option open to her family was to cut off the offending member lest it pollute the rest of the body. If she had come from a conservative Muslim family, she would have lost her life. For almost two years, there had been no communication between Haifa and her parents. It was a measure of Father's unusually humble nature that he had seized the opportunity and used Jim as an unwitting intermediary.

The telegram came on Thursday afternoon, and early the following morning, Father, Mother, Akram and Jim piled into the old Toyota and set off for Gaza. Elias, Akram's brother had arrived in Gaza with a Palestinian police company. The family hadn't seen him in years. Haifa refused to come.

They eventually found Elias seated behind a small steel desk in a little office in the police headquarters. He greeted them effusively, hugging and kissing his parents and his older brother and pumping Jim's hand. He proudly showed them his loaded Klashnikof rifle, his second lieutenant stripe and the authority accompanying it by ordering a passing policeman to make a pot of tea. He was witty, dominated the conversation and belittled what others had done so far. He assured them that he would soon be in a key position to straighten out the mess the Jews had left behind. Arafat recognized his superior talents, he confided.

Jim thought Elias attempted to cover his puny ego with a veneer of self-importance and contempt for others. He wondered how the newly formed Palestinian National Authority would get off the ground if all of its officers were Eliases.

17

Dancing

✦ ✦ ✦ ✦ ✦

S INCE THEY DANCED to different tunes, they couldn't syn-
chronize their steps. Yitzak Rabin moved to a carefully craft-
ed Twyla Tharp choreography. He combined familiar movements with clever gestures and abrupt, unexpected changes in
motion and mood. His seemingly spontaneous ways were carefully structured and flowed with mathematical precision.

Running, skipping, leaping, moving forward and backward
while hopping on one foot and making strange noises, the hon-
ourable Yasir Arafat, President of the State of Palestine, Chairman of the P.L.O. Executive Committee, head of the Palestine
National Authority and Commander-in-Chief of the Forces of
the Palestinian Revolution, got nowhere.

The odd couple made their debut at the September 1993
signing of the Oslo Accord in Washington. The media hype
surrounding the globally televised images of Arafat and Rabin
shaking hands on the White House lawn, followed by inter-
views with their beaming entourages, fed misguided hopes
that the two sides would harmonize their steps.

While Rabin went home after signing the accord, a confused Arafat had to keep dancing an impossible solo. But he was too old and too out of touch after twenty-five years of absence from the territories to dance to contemporary music. Shuffling pathetically to the complicated arrangements, he was unable to form credible Palestinian governmental and aid organizations, so little of the promised aid materialized. The revolutionary in exile who had molded his people's national identity into a coherent form became an incompetent authority figure. He lacked the statesmanship, maturity, wisdom and vision to lead his people through to independence. The hapless Arafat looked ridiculous and anachronistic, his movements sullen. King Hussein of Jordan, tired of waiting for the sluggish Arafat, signed his own peace agreement with Rabin. Even Arafat's close-knit circle of loyalists grew disillusioned by their boss' incompetence.

In May, Rabin and Arafat signed the Gaza-Jericho First agreement in Cairo. Broadcast live by satellite, the world watched as Arafat petulantly put down his pen, refusing to sign the map of the Jericho area. Only when Egypt's President Mubarak threatened that he would never set foot in Egypt again if he did not sign immediately did he grudgingly comply.

The Palestinian people, who had earned world-wide respect for their resourcefulness, their considerable achievements in education and their bravery in the face of an aggressive and powerful enemy, were stymied. A year after the handover, nothing seemed to have changed. Forty percent of the Gaza Strip was still under Israeli control, inflation rose to 20%, the cost of housing rose sharply and even posting a letter was a problem – Palestinian postage stamps were not accepted by the outside world. The legal system was confused, with Jericho applying Jordanian law while Gaza implemented the old British Mandate law. Both enclaves remained under Israeli military rules. In the rest of the West Bank, schools remained shut and the army continued to shoot stone-throwing children. The Palestinian National Authority was a foggy and confused structure marked by haphazard appointments, lack of accountability and devoid of a rational, consultative policy-making process.

The Palestinians turned against their Puppet-President. He responded by curtailing the freedom of the press and banning "all political meetings of whatever coloration" without prior written permission from himself.

Rabin regularly handed his partner large cheques with which Arafat could pay his multi-branched security and intelligence services. For the Israeli Prime Minister, everyone was dancing according to the script: Arafat was reduced to another Antoin Lahad, Israel's stooge "Arab leader" in its south Lebanon security zone. He had relieved Israel of upholding "law and order" in Gaza.

No one was impressed when the Rabin-Arafat-Perez trio received the Nobel Peace prize – least of all Hamas.

18

Hamas

✦ ✦ ✦ ✦ ✦

"TELL ME ABOUT HAMAS. Why does it exist? What is it after?" The tea house was quiet. Jim had lost the game of chess and was collecting the pieces.

"Hamas is the liberation movement of the Muslim Brotherhood," Akram's father replied. "The Brotherhood doesn't really seek liberation, however, nor does it seek to solve any problems; it merely intoxicates those who can't cope with failure. It is an expression of the hatred and frustration of Muslims who have been the prey of poverty and fear for too long.

"The Palestinian Muslim Brotherhood emerged in the 1970s under the leadership of Sheikh Ahmed Yasin as a cultural movement. Their goal then was to give an Islamic personality to the occupied territories. This meant that their struggle wasn't with the Jews, but with the P.L.O., whose 'atheistic commitment to narrow nationalism' they condemned. Both the Saudi and, believe it or not, the Israeli governments supplied them with money with which they built up a social infrastructure based around the mosque. The Israelis considered the

137

Brotherhood a counterbalance to the P.L.O., and as such were happy to support it.

"When the Intifada erupted in December 1987, the Brotherhood faced a dilemma. They could either strengthen their ties with the Israelis and lose street support or join the Intifada. They chose the latter. In 1988, they formed Hamas, which launched a series of successful guerrilla attacks in the West Bank and Gaza. These attacks, the fear they created, and Israel's expulsion of 423 'Muslim fundamentalists' into no-man's land between Israel and Lebanon in December 1992 gave them international notoriety. The Hamas onslaughts led to the bloodiest period of the intifada with mass killings, brutal repression and, let's admit it, to the severance of Jericho and Gaza from Israel. Hamas convinced Israel that it could never win in Gaza."

"If Hamas succeeded in that, why is it now trying to kill the rapprochement between Israel and the P.L.O.?" Jim asked.

"Hamas has opposed the P.L.O. ever since it recognized the 1967 borders of Israel in the Algiers Declaration of 1988. For Hamas, Palestine runs from the Jordan to the Mediterranean and is a holy trust that cannot be compromised. Though the P.L.O. claims to be the sole representative of the Palestinian people, the fact is that it is faced with violent mass opposition completely outside its control. Although Hamas has lost many leaders and numerous cells, they have proved their bravery and their organizational capacity. Many people support Hamas not out of religious convictions but because they don't like the path the P.L.O. is taking. The more Yasir Arafat fumbles, the greater the support for Hamas becomes." Akram's father sipped his coffee. "Arafat was more zealous in looking for that kidnapped Israeli soldier than the Israelis! We don't like the kind of peace Israel and America have offered and the P.L.O. has accepted," he added quietly.

"How would you feel if Hamas torpedoed the peace process?" Jim asked.

"Good."

Jim was startled, Akram's father bemused. "When the accords were first signed, I told you I felt like a man who had been robbed of a million dollars and was given ten in return. I could swallow that. Now that we know the nature of this peace accord, I feel like I have been robbed of a million dollars and then discovered that the robber is spending the money on my wife! That I cannot swallow."

A gust of wind smote the teahouse, causing the windowpanes to moan. Together they stared at the angry rainclouds rushing to cover the sun.

19

Jemal Karim

✦ ✦ ✦ ✦ ✦

SINCE THE FISH MARKET is next door, the Salaam restaurant on the beach near the harbour serves the freshest fish in Gaza. The waiter collected the plates, leaving Akram, Elias, Jim, Dieter and Jemal Karim to rub their distended stomachs. They gazed placidly at the workmen leisurely collecting their tools after a day's work on the new port. No one was in a hurry – curfews were a thing of the past.

"Jim, it's good to see you again," Jemal said once more.

"And you, Jemal," Jim repeated. He looked fondly at his old cellmate and rubbed his stomach some more. "Gaza sure has changed since I visited your brother two years ago," he sighed with satisfaction.

Jemal sat up. "What has changed, Jim?"

"No curfews, Arafat lives around the corner, Elias is carrying a Palestinian pistol on his hip and you have been released from prison. Look at that new dock and those fancy white buildings going up along the shoreline! I'd call that political and economic progress," Jim stated matter-of-factly. Elias nodded vigorously; Akram remained silent.

"Jim, you Westerners always measure progress in material terms. What difference does it make whether Arafat lives in Tel Aviv or Tunis. What difference does it make whether Elias Ibn Marwan or Yoshi Rubenstein carries the gun? The new dock and buildings merely indicate that someone is pumping some money into Gaza to create a dependent upper class that will resist any changes in the status quo. Sure they released me from prison, but Muhammed and Elias' own brother Tarik are still behind bars while the Jews continue stealing land from Arabs. In fact, the only difference between now and then is the lifting of the curfew. A small disturbance and Arafat will impose a new curfew which Elias Ibn Marwan here will enforce as vigorously as any Yoshi Rubenstein."

"Don't be a fool," Elias replied piqued. "Every country needs a law-enforcement agency."

"If Palestine is a country, so was Bophutaswana. Don't you see that the mantle of apartheid has been transferred to Israel? The Israelis have liberally granted autonomy to a new Bantustan!" Jemal said cynically. "Didn't you guys notice the new electronic fence they are constructing around the 'Palestinian Autonomous Area,' financed no doubt by the U.S.A. They who once criticized apartheid in South Africa now finance it for Israel. They even pay your salary, Elias. Listen, Arafat sold our birthright for a mess of pottage."

"You be careful about how you talk about our President," Elias said heatedly. "Your divisive talk is counter-productive. At this crucial time in our history, we must stand united behind our President."

"'Arabs of the World unite!' Let us unite behind our latest tyrant who will liberate us from the influence of the evil West and its Zionist lacky, both of which we secretly aspire to be like. Listen," Jemal added, "I'm tired of old slogans."

Elias stood up angrily. "You are a Hamas activist, just like your doctor brother!" he shouted, patting his pistol. "We'll crush you like a beetle." He turned and walked away, his eyes reduced to narrow slits.

They watched him go. Jemal scratched his head and raised his eyebrow. "Hamas activist... the new label for undesirables."

"Jemal, you came down hard on him. He is only trying to do his job," Jim said.

"Jimmy, what has changed?" Jemal asked. "Because of his type, I still cannot say, write or film what I want. They equate unity with conformity. That is what I rebel against. We should thank the West for cutting the 'Arab Nation' into palatable bits... What are you smiling about, Jim?" Jemal interrupted himself.

Jim's smile turned to a chuckle. "I was thinking of a conversation I once had with your brother."

Jemal laughed. "Yea, we see things differently. I don't fear Westernization, I embrace it. My problem with the West is that it offered us its false gods instead of its liberating values. You gave us nationalism, materialism, technology, Fascism and Communism instead of Aquinas, Voltaire, Descartes, Goethe, Tolstoy and Dostoyevski. Consequently, we are stagnating spiritually. Combine Western humanism with such traditional Arabic cultural values as hospitality, generosity, courage and honour, and you have heaven on earth."

"Elias was right. You are no different from your brother," Dieter said quietly. He hadn't spoken until now and they looked questioningly at him. "You and your brother are both running after the same mirage, the ephemeral hope of heaven on earth

– your brother through the imposition of Islamic law, you through humanism. Both of you will be disappointed since you both hope man can change for the better – you through education and Westernization and your brother through the imposition of brutal law."

Jemal turned to Dieter. "Man, you are pessimistic!"

"No, realistic. You underestimate the evil in each of us."

Jemal took a deep puff from his cigarette. "How then do you propose to change society?"

"By turning my back on it," Dieter replied. "I don't focus on changing society but on inviting individuals to step out of society to become disciples of Jesus Christ. Just as He turned his back on the spiritual and cultural values of His world, so must we."

"Christ was crucified for His efforts," Jemal replied.

"Exactly," Dieter smiled. "And that's how He effected the greatest revolution of all. He left behind a community of men and women who have turned their backs on this world, who seek only to worship God in spirit and truth and to humbly serve each other. That is the new man both you and your brother are seeking to create. But he cannot be created. He is personally chosen by God and he forms a little counter-culture of his own – the Church."

"You should enter a monastery." The corners of Jemal's mouth lifted cynically.

"Monasteries kept the spark of civilization alive through ages of cultural barbarity," Dieter replied intensely. "You look to us for values which we have long since proven to be bankrupt. Listen, Jemal, don't look to the West. It has nothing to offer. Your much envied humanism is a mirage, offering enlightenment but delivering apathy and runaway greed. People in our society care only about their own comfort. They retreat into small worlds of their own creation in which King Self reigns at the expense of the beautiful, the true and the lofty. They cocoon themselves from the grief and the gore of the big bad world 'out there.'"

Dieter began speaking with an almost fanatic intensity, as if he hated his own country. "Jemal, you've been to the States. Did you ever listen to the kids wandering the shopping malls, or to students in a cafeteria or to workers during their lunch hour? Instead of getting a decent education, doing their work well, raising their kids securely and helping the needy, they dismiss anything that intrudes on their boring, artificial little worlds with a yawn and a sigh. Our people are too lazy to open an atlas and find out where Palestine is, let alone be bothered to place what is happening in the world in a broader context. They are having too much fun on the merry-go-round of consumerism."

Jim could see Jemal fidgeting uncomfortably and, though he thought he basically agreed with what Dieter was saying, he was embarrassed at his roommate's outburst. Dieter, however, couldn't be stopped. He jabbed the air with his forefinger as he spoke.

"You know, Jemal, in some ways, we Bible-believing Christians have more in common with your brother than with you pseudo-intellectual humanists. To both your brother and to me, truth has sharp edges. Your brother's Islamic fundamentalism may be more bigoted, more frightening, but at least it puts God centre stage and holds certain things to be inviolable."

Dieter voice changed; he seemed to be pleading. "Jemal, forget about mapping your Arabic renaissance along Western lines. Forget trying to create a better society. Don't think in terms of society, think in terms of individuals, starting with yourself. Head for that church down the hill from Akram's house. Drive out those squabbling Greek, Catholic and Armenian priests, bulldoze the building and look for Christ Jesus, the Son of God and the Saviour of the world. When you've found Him, bow low. Then follow Him those eight kilometers up to Golgotha and He will take away your sin and make a spiritual man out of you."

"What good are spiritual men?" Jemal asked, barely able to mask his scorn.

"Only spiritual men know God, who is Spirit," Dieter answered. "And only men who know God can withstand modernity's barbarism," he continued. "Such men live in this world but are not of it. Like those ancient monks you ridicule, they create pockets of peace in tumultuous times. Through their families and their churches, they keep alive such divine values as love, forgiveness, honesty, unshakable joy and courage against evil. Spiritual men are the light points of civilization because civilization has no hold on them. Only spiritual men can break the spell history has on them and begin afresh."

Dieter stopped to collect his thoughts and Jim seized the opportunity to call for the bill. He and Jemal bickered amicably about who would have the honour of paying.

Dieter slumped in his chair. He looked tired. Akram gazed surreptitiously at him in admiration.

20

Black Friday

✦ ✦ ✦ ✦ ✦

THE FOLLOWING MORNING, November 18, 1994, started inconspicuously. In Jerusalem, Lieutenant Kahane arrived at work early as usual to read the intelligence dispatches that had come in during the night. One mentioned something about the possibility of an illegal Hamas rally after afternoon prayers at the Palestine Mosque in Gaza. He faxed it through to the Palestinian Police Headquarters in Gaza city.

In Gaza city, Jim, Dieter, Akram and Jemal woke up late and ate a leisurely, though somewhat stilted, breakfast. Jim was morose. He had lain awake that night thinking about Dieter's conversation with Jemal. He decided that he basically agreed with Dieter but, as happened so often, hadn't seen things in the same light and with the same clarity. He felt guilty. Instead of supporting his friend, he had cut him short; he had been ashamed of his friend's dogmatic outbursts before the suave, cultured Jemal. He also felt hypocritical; he had written Lois saying that he wanted to travel to the villages of Palestine with the good news of the gospel and then, when the opportunity arose, he was too ashamed to open his mouth.

Jemal was in a jocular mood. He had slept well and the morning mail brought him a royalties cheque from the T.V. station in France. He slapped Jim on the back and asked if Lois knew how grumpy he was in the morning.

Dieter was quiet and withdrawn. After breakfast, he retreated to a corner on the balcony to read his Bible and pray.

Akram asked to be excused to say farewell to Elias. They arranged to meet him at the bus station at midday.

Akram left the house and walked the few blocks to the police station where he found Elias engaged in a flurry of activity. Elias greeted him quickly and told him to wait outside while he briefed his men. Akram squatted on the ground in the hallway and waited patiently. For forty-five minutes, he watched the coming and goings.

Eventually, the door opened and several sergeants and corporals filed out. Akram entered just as Elias snapped his briefcase shut.

"Follow me," Elias told him. "I received an intelligence report from Jerusalem this morning," he confided. He was all purpose and authority as he walked briskly through the hallway to his office.

"Hamas is planning a major riot after the noontime sermon at the Palestine Mosque. I'm in charge of the operation." They reached his little office. Elias entered first, Akram followed. Elias sat down, pulled open a drawer and extracted a walkytalky which he clipped to his belt with dashing finality.

"My goal is containment and education," he continued. "We've got to prevent things from getting out of hand while at the same time teach these Hamas obstructionists that they cannot mess with the Palestinian National Authority." He looked at his watch and lit a cigarette. "Stick with me, Akram," Elias told his older brother, "and you can report the success of this operation to the family."

Several blocks away, Jim and Dieter thanked Jemal for his hospitality and headed for the bus station. They bought tickets, went to the teahouse next to the terminal, sat down, ordered Colas and waited for Akram to show up. They could hear the muffled, distant sound of the Imam at the Palestine Mosque haranguing the crowd without understanding what he said.

Akram never showed up. After they watched their bus leave without them, they decided to head for Elias' office. They were coming out of an alley to turn the corner toward the mosque when they heard a burst of gunfire. They saw a crowd of young men spewing out of the mosque. At the other end of the street, a Palestinian police jeep drove toward the crowd of youths. Dieter pushed Jim back into the alley.

"I don't believe my eyes," he said. "The Palestinian police are shooting Palestinians at prayer!" The jeep passed the alley.

"Look!" Jim shouted incredulously, pointing at the passing vehicle. "Akram and Elias!"

Elias was driving, Akram sat beside him and a third policeman rode shotgun behind them, brandishing his klashnikof. Another burst of gunfire echoed dully through the tangled streets and alleys. They stuck their heads around the corner to see what was happening. Instead of scattering before the jeep, they saw the crowd head toward it shouting, "Allahu Akbar." The jeep slowed down, then stopped. They saw the soldier in the back level his rifle at the crowd and fire again. Someone screamed and fell. The enraged crowd suddenly surged toward the jeep and started throwing stones. The jeep backed up, turned and spun back toward them. They could see the terrified look on Elias and Akram's faces. The soldier in the back shot into the crowd again. As the vehicle passed their alley, Jim stepped out, waved his arms and shouted, "Akram...!" The soldier turned toward them and shot. The bullet hit Jim in the chest, throwing him backwards against Dieter. The jeep increased speed dangerously, careening out of sight.

Jim crumpled in the dirt in the alley, his head propped up by the wall. A blood stain spread on his shirt, and his eyes grew large with fear. "Oh, my God, I'm shot, I'm shot! Diet, do something quick. Help me!"

Dieter ripped the shirt open. Bright blood frothed from a hole just below the left nipple. "Oh, my God, Diet, I'm gonna die, I'm gonna die..." Jim's breath was laboured.Dieter clamped his hand over the hole.

"You're gonna be all right, Jimmy. You're gonna be O.K.," he said, trying to collect his wits.

"Oh, no... Oh, no, Diet, I'm dying. I'm dying, man." Jim's breath came in short bursts. "It's not fair, man, it's not fair. Why is God doing this to me?" he panicked. The sobs hurt his chest, his breathing became more laboured, terror filled his eyes.

"He's got you where he wants you, Jimmy, crying out to Him."

"Pray for me, Diet. I'm afraid... I ain't ready to die yet, Diet." Jim's voice cracked and his chest heaved heavily.

"You're gonna be O.K., Jimmy. Just calm down. They'll be arriving with an ambulance soon."

When Dieter tried to lift Jim up he saw the gaping hole where the bullet had exited. He knew then that his friend would die.

"I'm scared, Diet. I ain't ready yet..." Jim's mouth moved spasmodically, tears smudged the dirt on his face.

"Yes, you're ready to die, Jimmy." Dieter looked Jim in the eye and concentrated on keeping his voice sounding calm. "Remember, Christ's righteousness is yours, Jimmy. He's taking you home early because he loves you extra much, Jimmy. Remember Enoch – he walked with God, then he was no more because God took him away." Dieter stroked Jim's face gently, smiling calmly, assuredly into his friend's contorted face.

"I was just beginning, Diet... I was just setting out..." Jim's voice faltered and his eyes glazed over. "I love you, Diet. Forgive me for last night... I love you, brother. I love you more than anyone."

"I know you do, Jimmy. Now just rest, Jimmy. There, put your head on my chest. That's it."

"It hurts, Diet, it really hurts." Jim's breath came in short, staccato bursts. He pinched his eyes shut and his head bobbed up and down with the effort of breathing.

"I know it does, Jimmy."

"Tell Lois I love her..."

"I will, Jimmy." Brightly coloured blood fizzed and bubbled through Dieter's fingers. Jim lifted his head, opened his eyes, smiled up at his friend, closed his eyes, bowed his head and sighed. The blood stopped frothing, then ceased flowing.

The crowd buzzed around them.

21

The Funeral

✦ ✦ ✦ ✦ ✦

IF MR. CAMPBELL couldn't have a gala wedding, he'd have a grand funeral. He and Mrs. Campbell, both dressed in immaculate matching dark blues, entered the sanctuary from the back and glided toward the place reserved for them at the front. Mr. Campbell, his face grave, gazed contentedly over the congregation as he traversed the length of the sanctuary. The building, packed with family, friends, employees, business contacts, well-wishers, faculty members, former fellow students and former students of Jim sat in religious silence, broken only by a faint sob coming from the front pew. The sunlight broke brilliantly through the stained-glass windows, throwing spots of brilliant red, green and navy onto the somber sea of dark blues and shades of black and grey. The organ played one of Bach's slow, majestic fugues. Mr. and Mrs. Campbell slid stately into the front row, bowed their heads and pretended a silent prayer.

A plain-looking working-class woman sobbed quietly at the other end of the Campbell pew. Mrs. Campbell slid gracefully across to the other side, put her arm around Jim's mother and smiled a melancholic, understanding smile. The congregation gazed upon her movement approvingly, some of the women wiping away a perfectly proper, feminine tear with their dainty handkerchiefs. Jim's father, a nondescript man, stared mutely at his only son, the pride of his life. His arms were folded stoically across his chest.

The profile of Jim's embalmed face was just visible above the decorative strip around the top of the coffin. It looked unnaturally white, the cheeks artificially rosy and the mouth twisted into a saintly, saccharine smile. The highly polished mahogany-and-copper coffin lying on the red velvet cloth on the altar seemed an integral part of the burnished pulpit and cross rising above it. A large bouquet of lilies lay in front of it.

On the right and left sides of the pulpit, a group of fresh-faced young men in funereal black suits, crisp white shirts and dark neckties sat apart. Because they were seated immediately below the pulpit, they had to raise their faces to see the speaker, making them look like the saints in Jan Van Eyck's painting, The Adoration of the Lamb. Mr. Campbell settled comfortably into the pew and nodded approvingly at one of the elders.

Suddenly, a murmur rippled through the church, disturbing the hallowed atmosphere. Lois walked in through the rear entrance and made her way to her parents. She was dressed in a beautifully tailored off-white dress, stunning in both its simplicity and in its stark contrast with the blacks, blues and greys which filled the church. She wore no hat or veil; her hair was tied back in Saxon braids. She slid into the bench beside her father just as the Reverend Dr. Charles Hendrikson appeared.

Dr. Hendrikson walked majestically from the side door leading to the consistory room to the pulpit, his huge black leather and gold-trimmed Bible folded across his chest. At the foot of the pulpit, he bowed his head in a moment of silent prayer, then ascended, adjusted the microphone and in his rich, deep voice, welcomed the congregation, expressing his appreciation on behalf of the Wilson and Campbell families to all who had come to express their sorrow and solidarity on this day. Then he invited the congregation to open their hymn-books to Martin Luther's great hymn of hope and victory, "A Mighty Fortress is our God." The organ played a few majestic introductory bars as the congregation shuffled to its feet.

During the sermon, Dr. Hendrikson was at his best. His deep baritone resonated comfortingly through the edifice, as he reminded all present of Jim's incredible physical and intellectual courage:

"James Fitzgerald Wilson was a man who was willing to pay any price – even the ultimate price – for the truth that in Christ there is no Greek or Jew. Our brother James braved wars and rumours of wars in that most tumultuous part of our globe, the Middle East, for the sake of the gospel. He willingly turned his back on a brilliant future, choosing instead to live a life of obscurity for the sake of Christ in order to share the good news of salvation in Jesus Christ with Jew and Gentile."

Dr. Hendrikson spoke with deep feeling as he described Jim's life: "Fearlessly, he ministered to both the enemies of Christ and to His chosen people alike. Like the heroes of Hebrews 11, the world is not fit for such as James Wilson, so God planned something better for him. He granted this brave young man the ultimate honour – martyrdom at the hands of the enemies of God." Rev. Hendrikson leaned forward and pointed down at Jim's corpse. "Dearly beloved," he said comfortingly, "that empty shell in that mahogany box isn't Jim. No, our Jim has joined that great select crowd of martyrs which stands before God's altar in heaven itself. As we read in John's Revelation, *those who have been slain because of the word of God and the testimony they maintained, call out in a loud voice, 'How long, Sovereign Lord, holy and true, until you avenge our blood?'* Dearly beloved, God will avenge His own!"

Dr. Hendrikson leaned forward and looked Jim's parents in the eye. "Jim's fervor and fearlessness inspires us all," he whispered in conclusion.

"Miss Lois Campbell, Jim's fiancée and daughter of our esteemed Mr. David Campbell, would like to share a few words with us. Before she does, the university men's choir, in which Jim once lifted his voice heavenward as well, will minister to us in music." The fresh-faced youths on either side of the pulpit stood up smartly and marched in step onto the podium overlooking the casket. A tenor briefly hummed the starting note before their voices joined in beautiful harmony as they sung "The Lord is My Shepherd" acapella.

As the final note echoed through the edifice, Lois stood up and managed to walk around Jim's coffin without looking at the body, something she couldn't permit herself to do for fear of breaking down in tears. As she climbed the podium, her stomach turned into a ball of nerves, her knees felt like jelly and she feared her voice would break. She sensed her father frowning questioningly behind her. Dr. Hendrikson gave her a sympathetic smile as she ascended the pulpit. She pulled a piece of paper out of her Bible, laid it in front of her, firmly grabbed the sides of the pulpit, took a deep breath and began. She looked at her father as she spoke.

"What actually motivated Jim and what does his death really mean to us?" she asked rhetorically. "Is he really a hero, a martyr, who knew what he wanted and was willing to pay any price to get it? Or was he merely a confused evangelical caught in a crossfire?" The congregation stirred uneasily. Lois' father's frown deepened, Jim's mother stopped sobbing and looked up at her questioningly, while her husband's dull glaze became a glare. Dr. Hendrikson nervously shifted his right leg over the left one.

"In Palestine, Jim was confronted with realities his theology, the theology of this church, hadn't prepared him for," she continued. "He met brothers and sisters in Christ who suffer because of our interpretation of the Bible.

"Jim may have been a confused Christian caught in a crossfire, but he was an honest Christian. For that I shall always love him," she whispered. She had to breath deeply once or twice to suppress her emotions. "When he realized that what he had been taught couldn't possibly be true, he was willing to pay any price to learn the truth – he was even willing to sacrifice me, whom I know he loved." She pulled a tissue out of her sleeve and wiped away the tears flowing down her cheeks. "Yes, Jim was a hero – not because he knew what he wanted and was willing to pay any price to get it, but because he didn't know what he wanted yet was willing to pay any price to learn."

The congregation relaxed, her father smiled approvingly, Jim's parents sunk back into the dull emotions of their grief while Dr. Hendrikson nodded sagaciously and languidly changed position.

"Whether or not Jim's death is meaningful or not depends on us," Lois continued. "If we fail to learn what he learned, he will have died in vain! And what did he learn? He saw us, you and me, as we really are: prejudiced, selfish Americans who have twisted the truth to fit our lifestyles, at the cost of the rest of the world. He saw a chauvinistic people under the spell of a truncated, militaristic gospel who believe theirs is the promised land." Her voice rose, the congregation stirred, her father's frown deepened and Dr. Hendrikson nervously placed one leg over the other again. Jim's parents, however, had stopped listening. Their grief had dulled their capacity to concentrate.

"Jim responded to what he learned by turning his back on us – on you and on me," Lois concluded, her voice wavering. "Let us ask ourselves what drove him to do so. Let us not simply return his body to the earth to go back to our old ways. Let us understand the effect our lifestyle and convictions have on our brothers and sisters in Christ in the third world and, having learned, let us reach out in love and self-sacrifice. Then Jim will not have died in vain." She picked her paper from the pulpit, turned and headed for her seat. She was depressed, knowing that her challenge fell on deaf ears.

Dr. Hendrikson jumped up behind her and adjusted the microphone to his height. "Thank you, sister, for those challenging words. Let us open our hymnbooks and turn to 'Blessed Assurance, Jesus is Mine.'"

The phone rang. Lois' father reached down and lifted the receiver. "Hello?"

"Hello, could I speak to Miss Lois Campbell please?"

"She went shopping, I believe. Can I take a message?"

"Yes, please. Tell her Worldwide Travels called to confirm her ticket to Tel Aviv."

"What! She ordered tickets to Tel Aviv?"

"Yes sir. In fact, I wondered if she was certain about wanting a one-way ticket? Just fifty dollars more will get her a year-long open return."

"Listen carefully, young lady. You cancel that ticket immediately, is that clear? I'll not have my daughter set off on some dangerous fool's errand."

"Er, could Miss Campbell herself confirm the cancellation?"

Mr. Campbell's face turned red. "Young lady, you do as I say," he shouted and slammed the phone onto the receiver.

The front door opened and Lois entered smiling. She was carrying two new Samsonite suitcases. She felt exquisitely alive.

Epilogue

✦ ✦ ✦ ✦ ✦

ON NOVEMBER 4, 1995, Lois checked in her luggage at Chicago's O'Hare International Airport, walked through customs and boarded El Al flight 795 to Tel Aviv.

At the same time in Tel Aviv's Central Square, Yitzhak Rabin was cheered by a giant peace rally. Together with his arch-rival and foreign minister Shimon Perez, he sang the "Song of Peace," a song often used against Rabin himself.

As El Al flight 795 lifted off, Rabin descended from the podium. Twenty-five-year-old Yigal Amir, a Zionist extremist, approached his Prime Minister from behind and shot him repeatedly at point blank range. Doctors later found the blood-stained paper containing the lyrics of the song Rabin had been singing:

> *Sing the song of peace*
> *With a mighty shout!*

When Lois' plane landed eight hours later, she stepped off the gangway and into a nation in trauma. The veil had lifted; the nation had caught a glimpse of its greatest enemy. That revelation nearly turned Rabin's martyrdom into a redemptive event. Nearly... That, however, is another story.

The day after her arrival, Lois ventured to Central Square. Standing among the crowds of mourners, she watched a jean-clad girl light two candles. The girl caught Lois' eye. Her cheeks were streaked with wetness.

"One is for the children he killed, the other is for the children he saved," she said.

Glossary

✦ ✦ ✦ ✦ ✦

Al-Fatah: Prior to the Oslo accord, Al-Fatah was the largest of the Palestinian guerrilla organizations. Today it is Yasir Arafat's "party" within the Palestinian National Council.

Anti-Lebanon: mountain range between Southern Syria and Lebanon.

Aoun, Michel: renegade Maronite general who led a failed coup in 1990.

Butrus Al Bustani: famous Syrian nationalist, intellectual and co-translator of the Bible.

Druze: An occult sect, an offshoot of the Ismailis which accepts the Fatimid Caliph Hakim as the final incarnation of God.

falafel: type of Middle Eastern "fast food" made of small vegetable rissoles.

Gemayel, Amin: former President of Lebanon.

hijab: the practice of veiling women from the sight of men.

kafiyeh: headdress worn by many Arab men. The kafiyeh consists of a piece of cloth and a black, twisted band which holds it in place. Palestinians generally wear a black and white kafiyeh.

mansaf: Jordanian national dish. It consists of rice, pine kernels, stewing steak or chicken pieces and yogourt sauce.

Maronites: an Eastern Church which reaccepted the authority of Rome in the early 18th century in return for the right to retain their oriental rites and customs.

mezze: meal consisting of plate after plate of hors d'oeuvres and various kinds of dips, purées, beans, etc.

Phalangists: Christian militia which operated in Lebanon during the civil war.

suq: market.

shoarma: type of Middle Eastern "fast food" resembling the Turkish Döner and the Greek Pita.

For more information or to place an order,
please contact your local Christian Bookstore
or:

103B Cannifton Road
Belleville, ON K8N 4V2

Phone (613) 962-2360; Fax (613) 962-3055
1-800-238-6376
Email: essence@intranet.on.ca
Internet: http://www.essence.on.ca

The following books are available from Essence Publishing:

A Sinner Meets the Saviour by Wayne MacLeod. . *85 pp, $8.95*
A study of encounters between Jesus and sinners in the Gospel of John and how these meetings caused people to re-examine and change their lives. This book will teach and challenge readers in their relationship with the Lord.

Olive Shoots Around Your Table by John Visser . *425 pp, $17.95*
Subtitled, *Raising Functional Kids in a Dysfunctional World*, this is a comprehensive manual on breaking the cycle of family dysfunction and raising healthy kids. Filled with practical insights, real life stories and helpful diagrams, this book is a must read for everyone who wants to understand the dynamics of family life.

Refiner's Fire by Reg Faust. . . . . *170 pp, $13.95*
This is the story of a man broken by the pain of rejection, abuse and his own failure and sin. Crushed beneath the apparant abandonment of God, he cries out in anguish as he loses both his family and his faith. Travel through the Psalms with this man as he searches and struggles through the fires of testing to find true healing.

From Tabernacle to Church by Dr. John Marcus. *156 pp, $13.95*
A deeper study of the Tabernacle and how it parallels the Church today in its service as the House of God. Contains many pictures and diagrams and study questions.

Handling Stress by John Visser . . . . *112 pp, $9.95*
To live is to experience stress. Some people cope very well with stress while others do not. This book discusses causes and symptoms of stress in today's world and gives practical advice on how to handle it.

A Lift for Living by Herman Kroeker . . . . *363 pp, $16.95*
A daily devotional for the whole year by a veteran servant of God. Filled with inspiring quotes, Scripture, prayers, stories & poems. Excellent for gift-giving & personal use.

And the Pink Snow Fell by Rev. Ray Cross . . . ***100 pp, $14.95***
This is the story of the Port Hope, ON, gas explosion of November 1993 and the huge impact it had on one of the families living adjacent to the site of the explosion. Contains many photographs. Excellent for grief therapy!

Protestant Church Growth in Korea by Dr. John Kim . ***364 pp, $39.95***
The Korean Church is one of the fastest growing churches in the world today. In this book, the author offers some insights into why this is so and examines some of the factors that have influenced this growth.

Controversy & Confusion by Herbert E. Holder . . . . . . ***275 pp, $23.75***
There are many different beliefs surrounding important doctrinal issues. This book addresses these conflicting beliefs and examines them under the microscope of Scripture to clarify what God really intended in His Word.

Binder of Wounds by Sini Den Otter . . . . ***129 pp, $11.95***
A medley of meditations describing some of the author's experiences as a hospital chaplain. Inspirational and honest, this book hopes to encourage believers in their daily struggles and give practical insights into caring for others.

Righteous Anger by Dr. Christopher Schrader . . ***180 pp, 16.95***
The negative effects of anger are reverberating across the entire global community. Examination of three examples in the Gospels and the opinions of various scholars give Christians concrete principles to follow for properly expressing anger — as Jesus did.

Whispers from Heaven by Gail Parks . . . . ***84 pp, $8.95***
A book of inspirational poetry that has touched the hearts of many people. It is the author's prayer that these words will encourage many, especially those who are suffering.

Order Form

Ordered By: (please print)

Name: _____

Address: _____

City: _____ Prov./State: _____

Postal/Zip Code: _____ Telephone: _____

Please send me the following book(s): (All Prices in Cdn. Dollars.)

Qty.	Title	Unit Price	Total
_____	*Desecrated Lands*	$12.95	$_____
_____	*A Sinner meets the Saviour*	$8.95	$_____
_____	*Olive Shoots Around Your Table*	$17.95	$_____
_____	*Refiner's Fire*	$13.95	$_____
_____	*From Tabernacle to Church*	$13.95	$_____
_____	*Handling Stress*	$9.95	$_____
_____	*A Lift for Living*	$16.95	$_____
_____	*And the Pink Snow Fell*	$14.95	$_____
_____	*Protestant Church Growth in Korea*	$39.95	$_____
_____	*Binder of Wounds*	$11.95	$_____
_____	*Righteous Anger*	$16.95	$_____

Shipping ($3.00 first book - $1.00 each add. book): $_____

G.S.T. @ 7%: $_____

Total: $_____

Payable by Cheque, Money Order or **VISA**

VISA #:_____ Expiry:_____

Signature:_____

**To order by phone, call our toll-free number, 1-800-238-6376
and have your credit card handy.**